Yesterday's Flight

by
Martyn Ellington

~ Yesterday's Flight ~

Contents

~ Yesterday's Flight ~

Chapter One

William sat down in his favourite chair, the old leather wingback groaned as he settled in to it, its soft leather shaping to his frame. The late evening sun glowed through the large corner window and bathed him in a warm light. He lifted his feet onto the table in front of him, took a sip of his coffee and sighed, closed his eyes and rested his head back. The TV was on, but he had no idea what show was on, no doubt it was another trash TV show targeted at the *young-have-it-all-now* generation, whose big emergency will no doubt be described by words such as *"like, you know"* and *"yeah"* which it seems is all they can muster these days. He opened his eyes and wondered if he was just getting old, or worse, turning into his dad!

Mustering the energy he reached for the remote, pointed it at the TV and pressed mute. Instantly he was in silence, the way he liked it, but he didn't want the TV off because strangely, it offered comfort.

Streaming pictures of the wider world confirmed to him that he was not so alone, even though he felt it most of the time.

He took a time check. "Shit," he thought, "I'm going to need to head out soon." Finishing his coffee with slow purposeful sips, he eased himself out of the chair, switched off the TV, picked up his suitcase and headed for the door.

William was an area manager. He had made his way slowly and sometimes it seemed painfully up the corporate ladder. He got there partly because of his sales ability and partly *(he liked to think)* because of his attention to detail.

Before closing the door he took one last look in the flat, satisfying himself it was clean and tidy, almost to the point of obsession, but he knew that upon his return in just a short 72-hours it would still be as clean and as tidy, and he could - with minimal effort - drop his case in the bedroom and relax back in his wingback with the soft glow of TV in the background. And with that satisfying thought in his head, he turned and closed the door behind him.

Bruce Ackland was a lead air crash investigation officer at the NTSB (National Transportation Safety Board) in Washington. Parking his car, he switched off the engine, leaned back into his seat and looked up at the grey, faceless building in front of him, he pushed his fingers under his glasses and rubbed his eyes. Stepping out of the car he wondered to himself what exactly this day would bring. He was weary and tired, he had just completed a 9-month investigation of a small private aircraft which had somehow managed to get itself tangled in some power lines.

"Why and how do some people learn to fly, with powers of observation that BAD?" he muttered to himself as he headed in through the main door.

Bruce was very good at what he did, but had a long career and decided a long time ago that nothing would surprise him anymore when it came to the reasons and excuses why planes and helicopters *'land in unscheduled ways'* as he liked to spin it.

Making his way to his office he could see that Simon had beat him in again, but then he should, he lived a lot closer and as he had been in the job nearly half the time, he was still eager to please and still found the excitement that Bruce had long lost.

"Bruce!" Simon shouted across the office.

"Bruce, you got back ok then?"

"It seems so, Simon," said Bruce.

"I'm pleased you're in, we've had a really unusual call come in this morning."

Simon sounded far too excited for this time on a Monday morning, but Bruce managed to raise at least some level of interest in his voice.

"Go on then, surprise me, another plane landed in the only lake for 500-miles, or better yet, hit the only tree for a thousand miles."

He looked up at Simon from behind his desk with a sarcastic look in his eye, "Oh no!" said Simon. "You're not going to believe this one, a team of palaeontologists working in Death Valley have uncovered what looks like a piece of tail from an airliner."

"Ok!" said Bruce. "Mike put you up to this?"

"No, really its real, and it seems they uncovered it while digging up the skull of a dinosaur."

Bruce dropped the look of sarcasm, and changed it for one of puzzlement.

"How can there be a tail section of an airliner lying next to the skull of a dinosaur?"

Simon shrugged his shoulders, "Dunno boss, but they say there is."

William was sat in the back of the taxi on his way to the airport. "Yet another sales meeting," he thought, "another meeting to talk about the last meeting we just had."

The voice in his head sounded frustrated, he hated red eye flights, long ones, flying from Portland to Atlanta was never a nice flight, it seemed to take forever.

"This is the last time for me, they don't know it yet, but when they've yapped their yapp, I'm throwing my notice at them, and that's me away."

He felt a smile spreading across his face. He had no idea what he would do, but he'd put enough by so that he could at least do what ever it was he decided to do.

The cab pulled up outside the airport. "Here you are, that'll be $22.87, bud."

William shuffled in his seat, until he found the pocket with his wallet in it. He handed the driver $25.00. "Keep the change."

The driver looked at him in a way that both thanked him and called him cheap at the same time, in return William gave him his best *'whatever'* look and climbed out of the cab and started to make his way through the revolving doors, clutching his overnight bag.

He'd almost made it in when he heard the unmistakable sound of metal smashing against metal and the dull sound of glass shattering. He turned to see the taxi he had just climbed out of being struck by a large SUV. The four occupants inside, two men and two women, jumped out and fled towards William, leaving the Toyota Landcruiser almost completely mounted on the bonnet of the now partly-crushed taxi.

William pushed through the doors as quickly as he could to get out of the way of the four strangers but he wasn't quite quick enough. The younger of the two men fell into William, knocking him against the handle on the door. Instantly William tried to push him back but he wasn't quick enough. With a hastily muttered apology, they were past him and gone. He watched with complete revulsion for them and their actions as they turned the corner and out of sight. As they did he heard the larger of the two men shout something towards one of the women, but all he could make out was her name, Andrea.

He made his way further into the airport and headed to the usual gate, smiling to himself as he noticed the airport police detaining the four people that had pushed past him just minutes ago. Walking slowly he dragged his case behind him, its little plastic wheels skipping and bouncing over the floor.

William approached the check-in desk and took his place in line, although it was a short a line.

"The only people who caught these red eyes are the people who have to," he chuckled to himself. Eventually he reached the desk and duly handed his case to the clerk.

William looked at her name badge, Becky, he often wondered

if that was ever their real names, or names some marketing focus group had decided people would trust more than the actual name. He stood looking at 'Becky' and waited for what he always thought was one of the most stupid questions he would hear in his life-time, and here it came. "Did you pack this bag yourself, sir? Could anybody have tampered with it?"

"Yes and no," he replied with a small smile in the corner of his mouth.

Becky looked at him and did what William thought only women can do, she rolled her eyes at him, without actually rolling her eyes!

He turned and made his way to the gate, catching his reflection in the tall mirrors, he looked at himself in his *off-the-peg* blue suit, the white shirt under it and the standard black shoes poking out the bottom of the slightly too long trousers.

He could never get the waist to the right length. William wasn't overweight or under, in fact his build, and everything about his features, were very unremarkable and very forgettable. He liked this anonymity, he liked blending into the background, not being noticed, being forgotten easily. He could almost hide in plain sight.

"One day when I have that fitted suit I promised myself," he muttered, "then I won't look like a bad mannequin dressed by a temp in a charity shop window."

He pushed his fingers through his brown hair; his hair was like the rest of him, a very standard short cut, no fancy styles, not for William. He was having a very good hair day if he could be bothered to put the side parting in on a morning, he liked to keep that for what he called special occasions. "At least my hair is not falling out," he laughed to himself, "not yet anyway."

He approached the gate and he could see the aircraft parked outside waiting for its cargo, which in this case were the passengers. He often felt like livestock being transported to the market or worse: the slaughter house. In fact a couple of the previous meetings he'd been to had felt very much like the latter, but not this one. At this one he'd have the last say when he said goodbye, it was the only reason William had decided to go.

He could have quite easily done this meeting by video link but no, this time he wanted the last say and he wanted it in person, so here he was boarding the red eye, flying half-way across America but it would be worth it, even if the triumph and glory of his departure would never be heard of outside the meeting-room and would no doubt be much more glorious in his head.

He showed his boarding card to another *Becky*, though this one was called Samantha. "No doubt another focus group name," he thought as he smiled at her, at least the best smile he could manage at this time.

He headed down the short tunnel and looked down the fuselage of the plane. He stopped, his foot hanging over the gap between the door of the tunnel and the door of the plane, "Welcome to flight 993 American Air Cruises, sir, sir, HELLO!"

William jumped back into focus and looked straight into the eyes of the flight attendant.

"Sorry," he said, "I was miles away." He looked at her name badge, 'Lynsey'.

"That's ok, sir, do you know where you're sitting?"

"I do, Lynsey and I even know where it is." His sarcasm was lost on her; she just smiled a flight attendant's smile and waved him onto the plane.

He made his way down the ever-so-familiar compartment until he reached his seat. He fell into it and looked out the window. By now the night had taken over, and the day was long gone and forgotten. His partner for the night's flight appeared next to him. She was a slim woman, he thought to himself, as she reached to the compartment above. She was wearing jeans, a red T-shirt and white training shoes. As she stepped back he looked at her and smiled. She pushed her blonde hair out of her face and smiled back, her brown eyes had a glisten about them as the cabin lights reflected off them.

"Hi! I'm Sarah, Sarah Talis."

"William, William Relford, pleased to meet you."

He tried to stand but could only manage a tilt out of the seat before she had sat down.

"I hate these red eyes," she announced.

William was already regretting saying hello now, he just wanted a quiet night. He wanted to rehearse his parting speech, over and over again until the delivery was to the standard of any great thespian. He imagined the scene. He would be standing at the end of the long table, the other managers clasping their hands and begging him not to leave as he stood heroically, a bright light shining behind him while he delivered his grand opus, not just for him but for all the people that have ever wanted to leave the job they hated. He smiled a little as a thought shot across his mind that the reality of course was that he would hand them his resignation and before he could start his delivery it would be accepted and forgotten as quickly as he would be.

"Penny for your thoughts!" Sarah said.

"Oh, nothing, just a little day dream."

She smiled and took a magazine from the seat back in front and started to read it.

"Thank God," thought William.

"Peace."

"Bruce, I've arranged the flight to Death Valley, the earliest I could get is tomorrow morning 10:00am." Bruce looked up at Simon from behind his glasses, "Ok, I'll see you at the airport tomorrow, seems a waste of time though. I'm sure these palaeontologist know their T-Rex from the, whatever the other dinosaurs are called."

"Raptor?" Simon interrupted.

"Well, whatever they might be called I'm sure when we get there this so-called tail section wont be."

With that last complaint about going registered, Bruce left the office. Simon shook his head and sighed, he couldn't understand why Bruce was so uninterested in this one. He looked up and watched Bruce leave the room, smiled, turned off the office light and left for home himself.

After an early start and sitting on a plane next to Simon becoming ever more excited about this mystery tail section, that will no doubt turn out to be nothing more than an 'interesting' rock formation, the last place Bruce wanted to be was in the back of a Toyota Landcruiser as it bounced and heaved slowly over the desert floor as it lumbered its way to the dig site; eventually coming to a stop 200-yards from the tape-protected mystery spot.

Bruce grabbed the door handle and swung the Landcruiser's door open. Immediately the cold air-conditioned environment they had enjoyed on the journey from the airport was replaced by searing heat.

"Shit! It's like opening an oven door," complained Bruce, but Simon was already out and opening the tailgate to retrieve his pack. Bruce looked at him, "You're just like a kid getting out of the car at Disney World!"

"Oh come on," replied Simon, "even you must admit, it's a bit exciting."

Simon had a shine in his eyes, a wonderment that Bruce remembered he once had from what seemed like a long time ago, back when doing what he did seemed exciting and challenging; challenging in a positive way, not challenging in a *"pain in the arse way,"* he thought.

Bruce climbed out, and started behind Simon, placing his baseball cap on his head, he could already feel sweat accumulating on the bald patch on the back of his scalp. He scratched at his thick tangled beard, "I hate the heat, no wonder these stupid things died out if they decided to live out here!"

"Actually the environment was very different during the cretaceous period." Bruce swung round to see who had corrected him whilst he was complaining to himself. "What?" Bruce snapped back, "This whole area was lush forests back when these guys were wandering around."

"Who are you?" Bruce replied with a note of *I don't really care and I don't want this conversation.*

"I'm Susan Lavey, one of the palaeontologists who discovered the tail section."

"Yeah, tail section, read a piece of freak rock, like one of those potatoes that are supposed to look like Jesus."

Susan looked at Bruce, smirked and walked away towards Simon, who seemed to be getting more and more excited.

Bruce started to follow he walked over slowly dragging his feet through the dirt, he really had hoped by this time in his career, field work would be a memory, and he would be sitting in a nice office barking orders out at all the Simons who run around excited and wanting to please like some new puppy wanting its play ball throwing so it can retrieve it and start all over again.

He pushed his way under the "Restricted Area" tape that surrounded the excavation. As he got closer he could only just make out the jaw line of something huge over the shoulders of Simon and Susan - who were squatted down, bending over the find.

He lowered himself down and pushed his way into the middle of them, then stopped dead, his eyes fixed straight. He tried to make them focus harder on what he was seeing. He wiped more sweat from his brow with the back of his right hand. The feeling of the sun on his bare neck was gone, he was oblivious to everything, the heat, the dryness, the noise of the dig, the dust that swirled around them, everything except what he saw in front of him.

He turned and looked at Simon, whose gaze was fixed directly ahead. He looked at Susan and she was staring right back at him, with a huge smile on her face. "Funny-shaped rock?" she whispered softly with a raised eyebrow. Bruce turned his gaze back and bent forward his hands; reaching out like some feelers or tentacles on the top of an ant's head as it struggles to understand its surroundings or looking for treats or food to take back to the colony.

He had to touch it because he didn't believe his eyes. He needed confirmation from another one of his senses, as if somehow his eyes had become untrustworthy and his brain wanted a second opinion.

His left hand reached out and made contact, he recoiled it instantly, but it didn't matter; he recognised immediately what he was seeing and what it was was the tip of the tail section of a Boeing 737.

He fell backward from his squatting position and let out a soft long sigh, as he clasped his right hand to his mouth. All around him seemed to go quiet, everything became surreal as his mind struggled to understand how and why the top 8ft section of a new airliner could be laid on top of the skull of a dinosaur from 65 million years ago, and what's more there were obvious impact points on the skull to indicate that this piece of aircraft had struck it, no doubt resulting in the animal's death.

Simon settled next to Bruce in the dirt. For once he was quiet, even with all his excitement and blind faith in believing what he had been told over the phone. He looked gaunt and washed out. Simon turned to Bruce, "You ever?" he didn't get to finish the question, he didn't need to, Bruce knew the answer and forced it over Simon's words, "No!" Both men were brought back to reality by Susan.

"We've got extra teams arriving tomorrow, specialist equipment to help us dig further, and we're going to widen the dig site."

"How long before you can dig down or further around or whatever you're planning on?" Bruce's question was phrased like a child asking when its mother would buy that toy she promised on her next shopping trip.

It didn't sound like the question a well-educated and experienced investigator would ask.

"A week, maybe two, your tents are set up, I figured you wouldn't wish to leave once you saw it," she said.

Bruce looked up, still dazed, "Oh, ermm, yeah ok, that's fine, thank you."

"I'll show you to them." Susan stood up and headed back towards the camp site. Bruce and Simon followed her.

"Here you go," Susan said, "they're both the same so whichever one you want is fine."

Bruce took the right tent and Simon the left, but only because that's how they were stood, at this point who had which tent was of absolutely no consequence and Bruce needed quiet time. He needed to get his mind around what he had just seen, and for that which tent he took wasn't important.

"Simon!"

"Yes, Bruce."

"Give me a couple of hours before I'm disturbed."

"Sure, boss."

He knew that tone and that look, Bruce was going into investigation mode. This was what he did best, digging the answers up, getting to what had really happened. Simon long suspected that Bruce was still doing field work so long into his career because he found it hard to do the office politics, he couldn't stand the corporate line, the *'blue sky thinking'* brigade, they all just annoyed him, clones with no real personality, but

Simon was confident, if anybody could figure this out, Bruce could.

Bruce folded the tent door closed behind him and the searing heat was known to him again. The rest of his senses started to come back on line, like some old computer that had been asked to do too much and had just frozen and crashed. Bruce's brain was starting to reboot, his systems coming back on line one by one, and the first one was telling him he was hot, too damn hot for his liking. He removed his baseball cap, and scratched his long thick beard. Rubbing more sweat from his brow he sat on the travel bed, leaned forward and put his face in to his hands and rested his elbows on his knees. Slowly his face emerged from his hands until they supported his chin. Bruce turned and laid down in one movement, put his hands behind his head and drifted into a restless sleep.

William could feel the plane starting to move, the little shunt bus pushed the huge aircraft to its starting position on the runway. It always amazed him how such a small vehicle could manoeuvre such a heavy object and do it smoothly and so precisely. The engines began to rev up and the cabin lights became that little brighter then flickered, "Here we go," said Sarah.

William didn't answer her. He wasn't a rude man, in fact bad manners were the only thing that was guaranteed to get the hairs on the back of his neck up, he just didn't want to encourage another conversation; instead he turned and gave her a listless smile, a kind of *"Yeah I know I'm sat next to you, please don't talk to me anymore,"* smile, and it seemed Sarah read it just fine. She nodded and returned to her magazine.

"Ladies and gentlemen, welcome to flight 993 Portland to Atlanta. I'm Captain David Padel and I wish you a pleasant flight. If you need any assistance, my cabin crew will only be too happy to help".

David had been a pilot for as long as he cared to remember.

He had gained his wings in the Royal Air Force flying first Harriers and then Tornados. After leaving the service he moved to America where he joined American Air Cruises. He had never married, he had always been too busy, never been stationed long enough anywhere to meet Mrs Padel, but this didn't bother him. Apart from his love of flying his other great passion was the gym, and between these two there was no room for meaningful relationships, and of course he loved his bachelor pad far too much to compromise on whether or not a pool table should be in the dining-room and do you really need all those Xbox games?

No, David was very happy with his life, and of course he had the added benefit of the cabin crew, some of who were more then happy to oblige.

One of those who were particularly happy to oblige was on this flight, Holly Danver, who had worked for the airline for 8-months but had soon made her presence felt on board by her huge character and *larger-than-life* personality.

Holly was only 5ft 6" and very slim but she had enough energy to fit into the body of someone twice her size. David and Holly had got together on their first red eye flight. It was brief as David remembered and not very romantic, but it was fun and energetic and surely that was the whole point, wasn't it?

David had a passion for red eyes and took them at every opportunity. It was always a quiet flight. The aircraft was always half-empty (or full, depending on your own take on that whole area), and most of the passengers on board would be asleep anyway.

David finished his pre-flight checks with his co-pilot and got the clearance he needed to take off. Pushing the throttle for the two under-wing jet engines to full, he could feel the battle between the thrust of the engines and power of the brakes. This was the part David enjoyed, the feeling of power he got from the engines and the feeling he got that he was in control of it all. The rest of the flight - once the aircraft was airborne - was merely a babysitting exercise for the on-board computers and autopilot. He released the brakes and the huge hulk started to lumber forward.

In the passenger compartment, William could feel himself being pushed back in his seat. The frame of the aircraft started to rumble and vibrate as it gained speed, quickly accelerating to that point of no return, where one fault, one mistake could and would spell disaster for everyone on board.

"Stop it!" he thought to himself. The noise of the engines increased to a tuneful screaming, then he felt the nose start to lift, the whole air frame tilting back and then the rumbling and vibration stopped; just the sound of the engines as they protested at being made to run at full throttle.

He looked out the window and saw the lights of the terminal and city falling away from him. He felt the plane tilt to the left, level out and then the engines went quiet. For a split second he daren't breathe. He was telling his heart to beat quieter as he listened intently for the engine noise that had suddenly stopped. He breathed a sigh of relief; and released his grip of the seat's arm rests, the engines were now humming happily rather screaming in protest.

"We've reached our altitude and the captain has reduced power," he reassured himself. The seat belt signs switched off and the LCD monitors in the back of the headrests flickered into life, giving him what seemed to be a never-ending choice of movies or lifestyle programming. "I wonder if *Snakes on a Plane* is on here," he chuckled to himself as he looked through the menu.

"*Avatar*, that'll pass the hours," he thought, and as at home he let the movie play to itself while he discarded the headphones, pulled down his blind and turned to sleep.

In the rest of the passenger compartment, most of the

passengers, like William, were now asleep; the only light coming from the dimmed overhead lighting and the LCD screens that were mostly playing to themselves.

Lynsey and Holly took care of the few passengers that wanted or needed attention and returned to their station to catch up on the latest gossip.

The 737 700 had 8 business class seats, but they were all empty on this flight, it seemed the people who had enough money to fly business class also had enough sense not to be on an aircraft at this time of the night. David checked the readings again as the plane corrected its path; checking itself and carrying out thousands of calculations a second, to make sure that at any given time it was exactly where it should be.

David sighed and rubbed the back of his neck as Lynsey brought him a coffee, "How are we looking, captain?" "Fine, Lyns, nothing to report here, I'm just holding her hand all the way home."

"Steve!" Lynsey turned to the co-pilot, "You want me to get you something?"

"No thanks, Lynsey, as it's all quiet in here, I'll head to the back and make sure all is ok."

The co-pilot unbuckled himself and left the flight deck to do his rounds, closely followed by Lynsey.

David turned back to face the dashboard to once again check the instrumentation; he knew everything would be ok, but partly out of routine and professionalism, but mostly boredom - he also knew it would run down another twenty-minutes or so, and as he predicted, all the instruments read exactly as they should.

He stretched back in his seat and looked into the black void that was outside his window. The only light was coming from the stars that always looked so much brighter this far up; so bright in fact that he imagined he could slide his window open and pluck one out of the night sky.

He smiled a little to himself and turned back to the instrument panel. It was when he looked down he noticed the VSD (Vertical Situation Display) which shows the aircraft's current and predicted flight path was now showing the wrong course.

David checked it and checked it again but the aircraft was off course and flying directly over Yosemite National Park.

"Shit, how could I be so far off course?" he said out loud to himself, then a terrible thought flashed through his mind.

This far off course could mean they would not have enough fuel. He felt his heart rate increase and his temperature rise quickly. He felt flushed and embarrassed like a child who had been caught out in class for forgetting his homework or not knowing the answer to a simple question.

That feeling came and went quickly as his training kicked in. Instantly he checked the HUD (Head-up Display) to verify the VSD, but it agreed with it. He turned to the EVS (Enhanced Vision System) on the aircraft to look for landmarks that he knew from previous flights and all the instrumentation agreed with themselves: he was off course - way off course.

"Shit, shit, shit," he shouted. "Piece of shit." He felt he had to blame something or someone. How could this have happened? he was too good for this rookie mistake; it must be the plane's fault, it had to be. All the instruments agreed with each other so it had to be. "It's that simple," he thought. "Ok, come on, you can do this." He tried to calm himself down and reached to call for Steve.

That was when he noticed the surface of his coffee rippling. Then the vibrations started, firstly through the seat, then the flight controls, then spreading rapidly to the dashboard. The screens flickered and went black, the HUD disappeared from in front of him, and the EVS went off like an old TV that slowly dies; leaving a little white spot in the middle of the screen. That was when he saw the light, just in the corner of his eye to start with, but it was there. He looked up directly out of the front window, a light starting to glow in the distance. He couldn't make it out, it reminded him of driving on a deserted road in the dead of night and seeing a single beam of light coming directly towards him, only for it to turn out to be a motorbike.

He snapped back to now. The light grew stronger and stronger, he turned his head and watched it grow in strength from the corner of his left eye. Shielding it with his open hand, he pulled his neck further into his shoulders. Suddenly the aircraft shuddered and pitched. It felt as though he was inside a toy aircraft while an unruly child ran around the home with it in his hand. It pitched backwards and up, the fuselage groaned and creaked under the strain, the light now all around the plane bathed it. It streamed in through all the windows blinding and hot, so very hot. David was powerless. He couldn't stop shielding his eyes to regain control. The dashboard was now blank. In the unnatural white light that surrounded them he could make out every screw head and every scratch and mark on the black dashboard.

Then nothing. As quickly as it had started it stopped. The light went, the pitching stopped, the flight controls and dashboard burst back into life and the master alarm sounded.

David took his hands away from his eyes and turned his gaze back to the windows looking out at the night sky, pitch black again. "Nothing...where are the stars?" he thought, but he had no time to think of an answer to his own question. The aircraft was already reacting to its latest threat.

The engines roared and screamed as if they knew their own fate and what would happen if they couldn't keep themselves and the plane in the air. Every display was reading incomprehensibly; none of them made sense, but he had to get the aircraft stable and level then he would find out what had happened and why the instruments were telling him lies.

The plane levelled out and the engines fell quiet, back to their normal even pitch. David looked around the flight deck for any signs of damage. He checked the damage control panel and all seemed to be ok. He uneasily breathed a sigh of relief, but it was a quiet one, a careful one in case whatever had caused this, whatever it was, was listening and just toying with them and his sigh would somehow enrage it and cause it to start it all over again.

He engaged the autopilot, keeping the aircraft in a holding flight pattern. It would endlessly circle now until either he could figure out what had happened and where they were, or they ran out of fuel!

"Fuel, shit!" the thought flashed across his mind leaving a white hot trail behind it. His adrenalin kicked in again, but by now he was almost out of it. He glanced down at the fuel gauges; they were reading 40% capacity, including the 9 auxiliary tanks, 4200 or so gallons left. "At this height and speed, that means I have..."

David was finding it hard to concentrate, the last series of events had seemed like a lifetime and yet had passed in just seconds. Nothing could have prepared him for it, not for the speed and ferocity at which it happened, not even his RAF training, not even the time he spent in the Falkland Islands when he was a Harrier pilot engaged in seek-and-destroy missions on the enemy Migs and surface vessels.

"C'mon, David think." He was finding it increasingly difficult to work his fuel out. His hand shook as he tried to recall the calculations.

"Think, ok, I have 4280 gallons remaining, that's roughly 26700lbs at this cruising speed and altitude. I need about 5500lbs per hour; that gives...c'mon...4.86-hours, ok!"

Knowing the aircraft could now fly in its holding pattern for a little over 4-hours; he unbuckled his belt and headed out of the flight deck.

Bruce folded back the flap on his tent and made his way back out into the intolerable heat of Death Valley. Simon was already at the dig site with Susan. Three days had passed since they had arrived at the dig site, by now the tail section and skull had been completely removed for forensic analysis and a further three digs had been started based on their best guess of the trajectory, laying angle and speed of impact of the piece of tail section they had found.

The dig sites fanned out in three arcs of 90° stretching as far as 500ft for the centre line and 250ft each side. The initial dig where the incomplete tail section had been found was now fondly known as *'ground zero'*. Bruce had commented on how Simon had coined the phrase remarking, "Trust Simon to think he's in the god damn X-File movie!"

He smiled to himself as he remembered Simon trying to disguise the fact and claiming he had just thought of it. It reminded him of how a child would either deny or acknowledge an event depending on whether they would be in trouble or not and be completely unconvincing.

Bruce made his way to the right side dig (dig alpha). The team there had found no more evidence or signs of what this could have been. "Mark!" bellowed Bruce. He had no time for small talk or making pleasantries. Mark was the team leader on dig alpha, a dinosaur fanatic, Mark did it for the love of being close to the remains of these animals that "Once ruled the earth and still would if not for the meteor." One of Mark's favourite comments on introducing himself.

Mark was passionate, almost to the point of annoying, but Bruce respected that, in his own field, Bruce was as passionate about what he did, even if he didn't show it and didn't want Simon to realise it.

"Yes, Bruce," replied Mark.

"You got anything yet? Found anything of interest? Anything that, say, oh, shouldn't be there?"

"Nothing, Bruce, not a bloody thing."

Bruce turned and headed for the central dig, (dig bravo) in charge of this dig was Andrea Sayer. Bruce despised this woman. Their first meeting did not go well. Bruce had remarked to Simon later in his tent that "If this woman cuts across me once more while I'm making my point, I swear they won't find her for another 65 million years either!"

Andrea was a boorish woman. She saw no place for manners or etiquette in the field. Her approach was simple and to the point, and whilst she did get the job done, she did upset a few people along the way; not that that mattered to her, but then that is why Susan had put her in charge of site bravo. It was beyond doubt the most likely to yield any results and for this it needed Andrea to drive it.

As Bruce closed on the site wiping yet more sweat from his forehead, he could see Andrea standing on the edge of the dig barking orders at her team. She was a stocky woman, 5ft 4", maybe 5ft 5", long black curly matted hair and a *'portly'* stance as Bruce had remarked to Simon. Her jeans were just a bit too long and dragged in the dirt at the back of her boots as she walked and she always wore that same damn white T- shirt and red checked lumber jack shirt.

As Bruce got closer he could see her stance change. No longer did she look like a Nazi guard patrolling the prison camp in one of those Second World War movies; where the allied soldiers had a duty to try and escape and the guards were all too dim to see the obvious tunnels and tonnes of earth falling from their trouser legs during the exercise break.

Now her stance had changed. She now almost resembled an owl or a bird of prey stalking its quarry just before it leaves its perch and swoops down. She stood almost to attention, frozen, her hands held up to her mouth, then slowly she made her way into the dig crater. As she dropped out of sight, Bruce reached the edge. He was just about to shout her to get her attention when he saw what it was they were all looking at and he too stopped dead.

Gathering his thoughts again he slowly made his way down into the dig until he found himself standing next to Andrea. "This is what I think it is, right? Andrea" "Yes, Bruce, it is." In the rocks, deep in the crater of dig bravo lay three human skeletons, buried purposefully and lined up side by side.

What made this grave all the more amazing and in fact worrying, was that they weren't bones they were looking at but fossilised remains, bones slowly replaced by the calcium in the rocks around them over millions of years until the bones themselves became rocks.

Bruce turned to Andrea, "How can this be? A piece of tail section found alongside a dinosaur skull and now this."

For once this tenacious woman was speechless, she just simply looked at Bruce and shrugged her heavy shoulders. "These are human remains? I mean, they are not early man, right?" Bruce was desperate for Andrea to tell him they were early man, not man, as we know him today, maybe Australopithecus or Homo heidelbergensis. Bruce thought of these two because they were the only ones he knew and right now he'd take anything, anything apart from what he already knew was going to be the answer. Andrea turned to Bruce and as she did, a chill tumbled down his spine. She didn't need to answer; he could tell by the look on her face. "No, Bruce, these are modern men - homo sapiens," she paused, "you and me, Bruce, you and me."

Time again seemed to stall as if on purpose; it was giving him time to take in what he was seeing. He had always had trouble understanding the time relativity law. A college friend had got the closest to explaining it to him one night in a bar in Massachusetts whilst he was at M.I.T.

"Put your hand on a hot poker and a second seems like an hour. Put your hand on a hot woman and an hour seems like a second."

But this was now, this vacuum of time that he stood in right here, right now, this was time-relative.

Suddenly his concentration was shattered, like a rock smashing through a pane of glass in slow motion. It was Simon, "BRUCE!" Bruce turned and scurried out of the dig running over to the third dig (dig charlie) where Simon and Susan had been working. He reached the edge and clambered down the side leaning back on his left hand with his body at an angle pushing his feet out in front, taking baby shuffle steps.

Bruce was not an athletic man. He loathed the whole gym working out culture. He really couldn't understand why people would pay what they paid to join a gym, drive there in the car, exercise while staring at the TV screen on the treadmill and then drive home again. He figured there are two elements of that he could do for free, drive home and stare at his own TV screen without the *'pain in the arse'* treadmill.

Bruce reached Simon, who looked even more excited than usual, but unusually he also looked confused. Simon turned to Bruce, "We've found what that the piece of tail section belongs to." Bruce looked down and there in the dirt, directly beneath his feet laid the outline of a Boeing 737, still mostly buried apart from the remains of the tail that was now projecting out of the dig.

Simon looked at Bruce, who had a look of utter disbelief on his face, his eyes visibly trying to deny the image before him, his mind clearly trying to *un*-see what he had just seen.

Bruce turned to Susan Lavey, "How long before this can be uncovered, Susan?"

"I'm not sure Bruce." She had a tone of uncertainty about her. Nervously she bit her bottom lip and turned to Bruce, "I don't think we're the right team to do this."

Bruce raised his eyebrows and looked at her with an expression of disappointment. "Look, Susan, until we know what's going on here, I think its best that we don't call anybody else in, just do your best and get this dug up or uncovered or whatever it is you say so that I can look at it."

Susan wanted to argue with Bruce. She was normally in charge and knew how to do her job well, very well in fact and she wasn't used to being spoken to like that, but she just nodded and turned away. The fact was, Bruce was right, they couldn't risk this getting out - not yet and she understood his frustrations.

Like her, he didn't like *not* knowing or understanding things. She stopped and turned back towards him. "Bruce, I know a guy, I've used him sometimes. He provides specialist equipment for large dig sites, we can trust him. I should call him, we're going to need what he has."

Bruce nodded but as she left he added, "So long as you CAN trust him, Susan!"

She didn't reply; she simply walked away and headed for her tent.

Bruce turned his attention back to Simon, who had now moved closer to the sunken aircraft. He stepped gingerly onto the left wing, its metal surface only just visible beneath a layer of very fine desert sand. "Simon, this is the main priority now, get everyone from site alpha and do whatever Susan tells you to, from now until I say; you work for her." Simon looked back, "Ok, boss."

Chapter Two

Lynsey and Holly were making coffee in the galley when the vibrations started. By the time the intense hot light hit them, and the aircraft lunged and pitched, Lynsey was already falling back, her hands clasping at the galley counter but they were unable to gain any purchase on its highly-polished surface.

The coffee she had been holding was now in full flight, she watched it as if it was in slow motion, the waxed cardboard mug tumbling through the air. As the coffee escaped, it formed three dimensional droplet shapes as it left the cup.

Holly was in mid-air, heading backwards, her arms and legs flailing and reaching out as if to grab at some imaginary rope that only she could see.

It was when she made contact with something hard that her sheer panic was soon forgotten and replaced by the intense heat and pain she felt as her left arm hit the wall-mounted fire extinguisher.

Her radius took the full brunt of the force. It snapped instantly, sending the most excruciating and agonising sensation she had ever felt radiating out.

Holly landed in a heap, and by the time her head had hit the floor and her eyes had focused on the blue carpet, with its red and yellow squares, the plane had returned to normal flight.

"Holly! Holly! are you ok?" Lynsey could see Holly sitting crumpled against the bulkhead. She sat against it and bent forward. Her blonde hair had come forward completely covering her face.

Lynsey could see her right arm cradling her left. Holly looked at her through her tangled hair; her eyes streaming, swollen and red. She reminded Lynsey of a small child who stood before her mother holding out an 'owie' hoping she could make it all better.

Holly slowly removed her right hand with growing fear in her eyes. She looked at the wound and Lynsey could see instantly the dark patch spreading across her blue blazer. Heading over to where Holly sat, Lynsey helped her to her feet and gently removed the blood-soaked blazer. The deep red of her blood contrasted sharply against the ultra-white blouse she had washed and starched the night before; to make sure it was as white and as crisp as it could possibly be.

Reaching for the scissors, Lynsey cut the arm of her blouse off at the bicep. Holly gasped and looked away. She couldn't stand to see the wound in her arm, the gash was deep, and Lynsey could see her bone and could see without the need for an X-ray that it was severed in two.

"Ok honey, it's not that bad; we'll soon have this cleaned and sorted."

Lynsey tried to sound convincing but she knew there was little she could until they landed and got her to a hospital.

"Ok, this might sting," Lynsey warned Holly, but only a split second before, she poured the antiseptic over the wound. She didn't want to give Holly time to pull her arm back and out of the way. The antiseptic stung. Holly recoiled the stinging sensation was intense; she imagined that this is how it would feel to be stung by a thousand wasps at once.

"HOLY SHIT!" Holly clamped her teeth and drew her breath backwards, hopping up and down and clenching her right fist as hard as she could.

"Ok, hon, nearly done. I'll dress it now and then we'll get you to hospital as soon as we touch down."

Lynsey finished the dressing and helped Holly to a seat in business class which was just through the curtains that separated the galley and passenger compartments.

"Now, you get comfy in here and I'll go see what happened and check on the passengers."

Lynsey gave Holly some pain killers, covered her with a blanket and left her to settle down in the soft leather recliner.

By the time William had regained consciousness from his deep slumber, the event that woke him was over and the aircraft had returned back to its normal flight but he could tell as his brain started to distinguish between dream worlds and reality that something had happened; an event had taken place because of the way the other passengers were behaving and because the oxygen masks had deployed. He had woken up to mass hysteria.

Sarah was sitting bolt upright, her hands gripping the arm rests, her knuckles shining red against her pale white - almost transparent - skin, sweat running freely down her brow. The oxygen mask straps that held it in place around her face were embedding themselves into her skin and leaving red lines against her pale complexion.

As William stared at her he could see her pupils increasing in size. He looked harder at her, she was almost taking on the appearance of a Manga character. A thought bolted into his mind. He suddenly realised that everyone was wearing their oxygen masks, everyone but him!

He grabbed at it and missed. He panicked and felt for a spilt second like someone drowning and reaching for a rope life-line that was floating in water but was just out of reach and kept moving with the surface movements.

Grabbing again he managed to catch it in his left hand pulling it furiously towards him he placed it on his face and started to breathe deeply. He put his right hand on Sarah's left hand to reassure her and her grip started to release. She turned to him, her face streaming in sweat. Her breathing was shallow and fast, her throat gagged as it tried desperately to get a lungful of air. She looked terrified and immediately they made eye contact.

She released her right hand and threw it around William's left shoulder; burying her face into his chest. She hung on to him like one of those baby monkeys William had seen on the National Geographic channel.

After what seemed an eternity - but in fact was only a few seconds - William realised that the aircraft seemed to be flying steadily and straight. He placed his right hand on Sarah's right hand that was attached to his left shoulder and gently pulled it away. "It's ok, ok, I think were out of it now." Sarah slowly lifted her head and returned to her normal seating position.

"Sorry, I don't normally dive into men's arms like that but errrrm, well, it was kind of, you know!"

The colour was slowly returning to her face and her eyes seemed to be back to their normal size.

"Don't worry, I think we were all a little scared by that, *that* whatever it was."

"Turbulence, sir."

Lynsey's calm and professional voice reassured and convinced them both with just two words, but she decided to continue with the mandatory corporate speak that had been drilled in to her during her training.

"Sometimes we hit isolated pockets of turbulence and it can have an effect on the aircraft as indeed it just has, but I assure you, these planes are designed to handle much more than that and everything is now fine."

She smiled at them both, just for a little extra encouragement, and moved on to the next passengers.

"There we go, Sarah, nothing to be worried about, just a little turbulence.

"If that's little I'd hate to go through gigantic!"

William smiled and although he wanted a quiet flight, the idea of turning his back on her now seemed contradictory to his self-imposed high standards of manners. He hung his gaze on Sarah for a little while longer and smiled softly, "I think it's time for a drink."

David made sure the flight deck door was secured and locked when he left. He made his way back through business class and pulled the curtain back that led into the galley. As he did he could see Lynsey helping Holly on the other side.

Lynsey had her back to him and although he wanted to go across and offer what help he could, he knew that he needed to ensure the air frame was intact. He turned to his left and pressed the button that summoned the lift that would take him down into the cargo hold. Once in place he opened the door and pressed the descent button. The lift jumped and started its short trip down under the passenger compartment. There was a clunk and the lift settled in place. He opened the glass door and stepped out. In the cargo hold he could hear the steady reassuring hum of the under-wing engines. He placed his hands on the fuselage and felt a comforting gentle vibration.

He knew, through years of flying, if an aircraft was sick a good pilot could not only hear it, but he could feel it as well and at this point the aircraft felt fine. He gave the metal a gentle tap as if to say well done - like you would a faithful dog after giving it treat.

He sighed and moved forward. "We were lucky down here," he thought; everything seemed to be tied down and secured.

He moved to the avionics bay. Entering, he had a cursory look around, though this was Steven's department, really, everything looked fine. "No alarms or red flashing lights, I'm happy with that," he said softly to himself.

He turned and headed back out of the avionics bay with a satisfied smile on his face, reflecting his good fortune so far in his inspection. He turned to carry on and then stopped in his tracks, "Steve?" he was calling out to the black shoes that were sticking out from behind the last bulkhead, "Steven?" He shouted towards them then the thought dawned on him, he'd been so preoccupied with everything that had happened in the few minutes, looking for Steven, his co-pilot hadn't even occurred to him. He started forward and turned behind the last bulkhead at the rear of the aircraft and found himself looking down on his co-pilot. His body was lying limp and David could tell instantly that he was dead. He had seen enough dead bodies while serving with the RAF in the Falklands to know.

He looked at the lifeless body in front him. His legs seemed to be how they should be, but it was when his gaze reached his upper body that David pulled away and turned his head.

Regaining his composure, he knelt down next to him. He had to feel for a pulse, though he knew it was pointless. Steven's left shoulder was completely dislocated; his arm lying at an unnatural angle across his body like a discarded rag doll that had been thrown to the floor when it no longer held any pleasure for the child playing with it. As he suspected there were no signs of life, his head was turned at an impossible slant, his lifeless eyes were dull and had a glaze over them and the colour in them had all but disappeared. They looked blankly towards the ceiling in the cargo bay, the skin around his neck didn't seem to fit, like a badly wrapped present that was an awkward shape, there just seemed to be too much of it.

He could make out the shapes of vertebrae as they protruded under the skin as if they were trying to find a way out. The skin was gathered and nipped and was already turning a dull yellow colour. David surmised that Steven must have been thrown across the cargo bay during the *'event'*.

He had hit the corner of the bulkhead, dislocating his shoulder and moments later snapped his neck on the support bar of the passenger compartment. The last thing he would have seen was the ceiling as he flew through the air.

David reached over and pulled his eyelids shut and then did the only thing he could with the body, he simply secured it and covered it. He stood for a short while. He didn't offer any prayers. David was not a religious man, he had no faith in the traditional sense and had no feelings for any greater powers or almighty beings that play with us for their own amusement.

He wasn't really sure what he should say or do. He didn't really know Steven, he had only flown with him once before when he was training. He seemed ok, a nice guy he had thought, but beyond that he had no thoughts or opinions on him, in fact when asked his opinion by the instructor, David had simply said, "He seems ok, he knows what he's doing, I guess. What's my thoughts? I don't have any; I kind of know nothing of him!"

At that, his thoughts turned instantly back to the aircraft now flying itself in a circular holding pattern above Yosemite National Park.

With a heavy sigh he pushed himself back to his feet and headed for the lift that would take him up to the passenger compartment. He stepped out of it into the galley and stepped back in to business class where he saw Holly resting, covered in a blanket.

"Sorry, captain," she said softly - half smiling and half wincing.

"What happened to you?" he asked.

"I got thrown across the galley when we hit that turbulence," Holly said. "I've broken my arm, but I wasn't brave enough to look at it."

David gave her his best, *You'll be fine,* smile and headed back onto the flight deck. He sat back in his seat and took a deep breath. He placed his headset on. "Mayday! Mayday! this is flight 993 American Air Cruises, we have hit bad turbulence and sustained casualties over..." *sccchhhhhhhhhh...*

He heard nothing but static. "I say again, Mayday! Mayday! This is flight 993 American Air Cruises, we have hit bad turbulence and sustained casualties over..."

Still nothing. He pulled his headset off and looked at the dashboard to check the flight and fuel status.

After checking on the few passengers they had on board and doing her best to reassure them, Lynsey returned to Holly to see how she was holding up; she knelt quietly down beside her and found her asleep, Lynsey smiled and pulled the blanket further over her. She looked peaceful and restful; a sharp contrast to how she had been a while ago. She carefully lifted the edge of the blanket that covered her left arm, the bandage was holding and the bleeding had stopped but she could see the bruising starting to radiate from the fracture area. Lynsey gritted her teeth and drew a breath back through them, "That's gotta hurt, sweetie," she whispered to herself as she covered her over again and stood up, turned and headed for the flight deck.

"Captain, how are things in here?" Lynsey walked slowly in. She was tired now and drained, a bit like Holly but unlike Holly, she couldn't yet take a rest.

Due to cutbacks at the airline they had decided that any flights with less than thirty-five passengers, and this particular red eye had only eighteen, would only need two cabin crew and two flight officers. With Holly out of action, that left her to carry the load.

Lynsey sat next to David and turned to look at him, "Where's Steve?" David looked down before he turned to face her, his expression a mixture of sadness and inevitability, he simply gave a small movement of head and whispered, "No, he didn't make it." Lynsey covered her mouth with both hands and gasped. Her eyes filled up instantly as if someone had turned on a tap, tears began to stream down both her cheeks; carrying with them her black mascara. Removing her hands from her mouth she stuttered, "How? Where?"

"In the cargo hold, broke his neck, it would have been instant."

David looked down again and away from her.

"We, we," she stuttered again, "we need to inform the airline."

"I can't, I can't get anybody on the radio, it's as if there is no one out there, the instruments aren't reading anything; no GPS, nothing on radar; just nothing and look, I've been looking at the night's sky. I've flown this route time and time again and I don't recognise the sky even though we're off course I should still be able to see familiar scenes.

Lynsey's tears had stopped, her anguish now replaced with a sense of concern.

"So, what does that mean?"

"Honestly, I don't know, Lynsey, I reckon we have 3-hours of fuel left in this holding pattern and the sun should be up in 2-hours, so that gives me an hour of daylight to find something or," he paused, "somewhere to land."

Lynsey sat back in the co-pilot's seat.

"So, what do we tell the passengers?"

David looked at her and shrugged his shoulders.

The plane continued its circling. David and Lynsey sat in silence, the relentless static was still coming over the radio speakers and was now just becoming yet a another background noise, dissolving into all the other sounds that can be heard in the flight deck but are so easily ignored.

As the day started to break the sun broke through the windows of the flight deck streaming in and bathing David in a warm light, but this light was different from the scolding pure white light he had experienced the previous night, this warmth was very welcome, and just for a small moment he allowed himself the luxury of enjoying it.

He rubbed his face and breathed deeply as if he was showering in it. Lynsey had continued to come in and out, continually checking on Holly and the passengers. On this visit she brought him a coffee. David placed it down in the usual spot but before he let go of the handle he took a second and had a flashback to the last coffee that was there and saw again the vibrations on the surface just before the event had happened.

He blinked hard and realised it was just a flashback, sighing heavily and smiling he looked up and smiled at Lynsey.

"Thanks Lyns, how's things out there?"

"Oh, as well as can be expected. Holly is resting, but her arm is bruised really badly, and the passengers are ok-*ish,* thankfully none of them have noticed we're circling for now."

"For now," David replied, "but the sun is up and now they have landmarks to look at."

"How we doing for fuel?" Lynsey asked the question but she really didn't want to, it was the same kind of feeling she had the last time she rang her credit card company for a balance, she knew she had to ask but she dreaded the answer.

"We have about 45-minutes, Lynsey, its time to find a place to land."

She looked at him and sighed, she had a look of acceptance on her face. Lynsey wasn't a pilot but she had worked for the airline and flown enough times to know what was about to happen, and she knew that what was about to happen was an emergency landing. She looked one last time at David, nodded and stepped out.

"Ladies and Gentlemen, this is the captain speaking. Due to circumstances that we don't fully understand, I'm afraid to inform you that I am going to have to make an emergency landing. Lynsey our senior flight attendant will soon be round to ensure you are all aware of what to expect. Unfortunately, Holly was injured in the turbulence and won't be able to assist any further."

David started to bank the plane, taking manual control of it again he disengaged the auto pilot. The on-board computers had done their job now and as clever as they were and good as they were, it was time for the human touch. He started to scan the horizon looking for familiar landmarks, but nothing of what he saw down there looked familiar. He expected to see the national park but instead all he could see for as far as he could were thick lush forests. He felt the adrenaline kicking again, but this time he got it under control, this time he was going to control it. He figured he had around 30-minutes of fuel now and that was barely enough to do what he had to do. He had to find a strip of land and now.

He banked left and found what he was looking for, he had no choice he had to make a decision and he had made it, that was where he was going to land, or to be accurate it: where he was going to make a controlled crash. He knew he was going to need all the 900-metres this aircraft needed and depending on the conditions of the improvised landing strip, even that might not be enough. He turned the aircraft and started to make his approach.

Bruce was in his tent; he had just woken up, they had been here two weeks now, and he had hated every day more than the last. He hated the heat but worse was the dust. God, he hated the dust.

He was perched on the edge of his bunk resting his elbows on the sides of his knees; his head supported by his hands. The early light of Death Valley was streaming in through the yellow canvas as was the smell of freshly-brewed coffee. He rubbed his hands over the top of his head and stood up stretching out as if he was reaching for something.

"Bruce, are you decent in there?"

"I'm dressed, Susan but it's too damn early for me to be decent about anything!"

Susan laughed, she was used to his rough demeanour by now, especially this early in the morning and she could tell from his reply that last night had not been a good night for him.

"Come on, Bruce, we've finished looking at the first two bodies from dig bravo."

Bruce steadied himself and stepped out the tent. 8:37am, his watch read, sighing heavily he looked at Susan through squinted eyes as they got used to the sun that already started to annoy him.

"Why this early, Susan?"

She just smiled and turned, "C'mon, let's go see."

"Not without a coffee, that's first, those fossils can wait for another ten-minutes."

"I'll meet you over there then."

Susan walked off and Bruce headed for the kitchen tent.

With his morning coffee in one hand and his other hand over the top of the cardboard cup to stop any spilling or escaping before he had chance to drink it, he made his way slowly over to the large field examination tent they had erected over dig bravo.

As he walked in he could see Susan standing over the examination table they had put the first two bodies on.

"So, what can you tell me about John and Jane Doe here?"

Susan turned her head over her shoulder and smiled, she didn't need to turn completely around, she could recognise that voice anyway.

"Well, as you know, one's male and the other female, what we have established is that John here, has a dislocated shoulder from a heavy impact, but the interesting thing is how he died.

"Go on," said Bruce, as he sipped a little more coffee, "His neck is very badly broken, you see here just below the skull it suffered a massive impact from behind him, so we're not too sure what caused it but it's a safe guess to say he didn't see it coming."

Bruce held his coffee out to one side so he couldn't dribble any on the bodies.

He was now bent over, partly out of respect for them, partly because he needed every drip of caffeine to get him started but mostly because it would be just plain embarrassing.

Susan held her pen close to where the point of trauma had taken place, and even though they were fossils now, he winced as he imagined the force that his neck must have taken.

"Do you think someone did that?"

"I doubt it," Susan replied candidly, "it would have taken a big man to do that, the object - whatever it was - was brought down on him, and given his height at around 6' they would have needed to be much bigger or standing on something to get the elevation."

Bruce turned to the female remains.

"Ok, what about Jane here?"

"Ah, she's more interesting. You can see her left arm had a bad break of the radius bone, and it seemed it never healed before she died."

"What could have caused it?"

"Again, its just best guess, but as with her friend here what ever it was, there was force involved."

Bruce moved closer in for a detailed look. Turning to Susan he shrugged his shoulders, "So, what do you think killed her then?"

"Well, forensically we can tell she died while she was still young and the break in her arm wasn't that old; we can tell that by the stage the bone is at in the healing process. Our best guess is that the trauma to the area must have allowed some kind of infection to get in and ultimately she died from some sort of septicaemia poisoning."

Bruce stood up and looked bewildered.

"What is it?" Susan asked. "These two fossils here were once modern people, who we think are off that plane over there that shouldn't be; yet they died from traumatic injuries and bad infections around 65 million years ago."

Susan just stared at him, "I don't know what else to tell you Bruce."

Bruce pulled in a deep breath to fill his lungs then let out a heavy sigh. "Tell me, is there anyway at all these people can be identified?" Susan looked at him with a look of excitement growing across her face, like someone who was opening a present and starting to realise that what was in under all the wrapping paper was the thing they had wished for. "You know, we just might be able to, there has been work done in the past to restore the faces of Homo heidelbergensis and other early man, they weren't anywhere near as old as these but they might be able to do something."

"Ok, Susan, get in touch with whoever it is that does this and tell them it's a priority."

He turned from the table and headed to the mass grave where the other body still laid; squatting down he stared at it intensely. "I have a million questions for you and you can't help." Raising himself back up and gulping down the last of his coffee he headed for dig site charlie to see what further work had been done on the remains of the aircraft since Bruce had last seen it 24-hours ago.

They had first discovered the plane just over a week ago. Susan's contact had provided the equipment they just couldn't have done without, but Bruce still wondered at what cost and if he could be trusted as much as Susan insisted he could.

Bruce approached the dig site - which, as with the other two sites - now had a huge tent over it, covering the remains of the aircraft.

Entering it, Bruce could see the half-excavated plane, its paintwork was badly marked almost scratched down to the bare metal, years of erosion from sand, earth, water and high winds had scratched off all the markings and corporate livery that had no doubt once announced to everybody who saw it what it was and who's it was. Huge powerful orange lights illuminated the entire area. Because of the strength of the sun, they had taken the decision to protect it, the canvas covering it was a dark blue; unlike the other sites which were white to maximise the available daylight, and out here there was a lot of daylight.

The 'aircraft hangar' - as it had now become affectionately known - was also air-conditioned. It was strange walking into this self-sealed environment from the scorching desert outside. In here it was cool and everything was immersed in an eerie orange glow. The half-visible plane and especially its tail even with the missing section was rising out of the desert floor like some huge leviathon rising out of the depths of the sea in Greek mythology.

Bruce looked around for Simon, who was running this dig now under Susan's stewardship, and given his huge amounts of energy and excitement for the whole thing he was making good progress. They had dug down far enough to know that the aircraft was sealed up, all the exterior doors had been closed and all the window blinds had been drawn down, tantalisingly they could not yet see into it.

Bruce noticed Simon standing by the forward entrance door on the left side of the fuselage; just behind the flight deck windows and in front of the row of small windows that once allowed the passengers behind them to gaze 'sometimes in wonder' he thought, at the earth below them.

"Simon!" Bruce shouted as he nodded his head up to get an extra few decibels out of his already booming voice.

Simon turned slowly, his left hand fixed steadfastly to the door and his right hand on his hip.

Bruce walked over to him and took a perspective look at Simon and smiled. Suddenly Simon didn't look like the over-eager, sometimes annoying and awkward young man that he climbed out of the Landcruiser with those two weeks ago. Now he looked like a fully competent and capable field investigator.

"Hi! Bruce, come and see this." He removed his hand from

his hip, something Bruce was glad about.

"Now he doesn't look like a teapot," he chirped to himself. Bruce reached the dig, looking down into it he could now see the bare tops of the wings and more importantly he could see that the landing gear was down from the earth the team had cleared away underneath it.

Bruce looked at Simon, "It landed?"

"Yup, and looking at the structure of the under carriage it was a controlled landing."

Bruce crossed his arms across his chest and rubbed his thick tangled beard. "What's the puzzle, Bruce?" Simon had been on enough field trips with Bruce to know what this look meant, and what it meant was that Bruce was stuck, he had a question that couldn't be answered, and that wasn't something he liked.

"Simon, have you looked at the aircraft?"

Simon looked at him, puzzled.

"Ermm, I have, I am now."

"No, Simon, have you really looked at it?"

Simon took a step back and looked as far as he could along the length of it.

"You still don't get it, Simon, do you? You still haven't yet seen the biggest question we should be asking!"

"Ok, Bruce, I give up, what is the biggest question we should be asking? You tell me."

Bruce pointed in the general direction of the grave.

"What's happened to the remains of what we think are a few of the crew or passengers?"

Simon frowned and bit his bottom lip, "They fossilised!"

"Ok," said Bruce, "And why did they do that?"

"We think, because of the time they have been down there, but until we get the carbon dating back from John Doe tomorrow..."

Bruce cut across his words, "Don't over think it, Simon, we

pretty much know it's about 65 million years and the first thing...the very first thing (Bruce's voice was raising now because he was getting frustrated) we saw was the skull of some animal that had been killed by this plane and that lived 65 million years ago."

Bruce rolled his hands as if to encourage Simon's thought-process.

Simon stood back, his faced panned into a solemn expression as if he had turned to stone on the spot. It was an expression that Bruce had not seen since they first saw the tail piece of the plane lying on the skull. He turned slowly to Bruce, "I need to call a team." Bruce smiled and just nodded. Simon had finally understood what Bruce was driving at.

The thing that everyone had missed, because they had been so busy trying to uncover the aircraft, they had missed the most obvious question: why had the plane not disintegrated? By now the air frame, metal, glass and even the plastics should have decomposed, but they hadn't. The plane was dirty, it had been buried over time as all artefacts and remains are, it would never fly again and there were signs of rust and decay, but it looked like an aircraft that had been left out for fifteen, maybe twenty years, not 65 million years.

Bruce started his way back out the hangar. He stepped out of the orange air-conditioned environment back into the baking midday sun. He pulled his baseball cap out of his back pocket and tucked it on his head.

Back in the hangar Simon took his phone out of his pocket and called the office.

"Hi! It's Simon at the Death Valley site, I need a metallurgy team down here, I have a plane that..." he paused..."That shouldn't be anything but a pile of dust!"

Chapter Three

D avid took a firm hold of the throttle in his right hand and held on to the control column with his left, none of the usual landing aids were working, he was flying completely manually; all he had was his judgment, experience and the altimeter. He could see the large clear grassy area in front of him, he lined the aircraft up. "Ok, you can do this, this is easy." He settled himself for the emergency landing. He could see the trees coming closer and faster, he knew he had to lower the landing gear at the last possible moment. Because of the approach angle there was a real danger of the trees taking them clean off. Looking at the fuel gauges he had only enough for one approach, if he over shot it he knew he would run out whilst trying to get airborne again.

He was getting close now, he could feel his heart rate rising, it felt like it was about to burst from his chest; his hands tightened their grip and he curled his toes inside his shoes as if to make sure his feet would work when he needed all the braking power he had at his command.

The ground was getting closer and faster; he felt the blood rushing around his body. He clenched his teeth and took a deep breath. The trees passed by the cockpit windows at a fantastic speed, he was now directly over the clearing. He pulled the nose up and lowered the landing gear, he heard the whining of their motors and then the click as they locked into place, his approach angle was extreme, he was almost at stall speed but he had to, he couldn't hit the grass at the same angle and speed as a normal runway.

Just as he thought he had cleared the last of the trees from the back of the aircraft, he heard a crashing sound and the airliner shuddered and pitched, the master alarm sounded and the hydraulics started to fail. He knew he had to get this plane down and now!

He fought and managed to get it back under control. There was no time and no fuel for another attempt if he got this wrong they would all be dead, the aircraft would hurtle into the woods on the other side of the clearing and he had seen too many news bulletins to know what a plane looks like when it does that.

The rear wheels hit the ground hard, the shock absorbers on the landing gear plunged into themselves taking the full weight of the plane in one hit. The plane bounced, and shuddered, the fuselage groaned and creaked, he used all his strength pushing the control column forward forcing the nose down. The front wheel hit the grass and the plane vibrated and shook as it hurtled along the ground; its wheels tearing up chunks of earth as they tried to dig in and sink under the immense weight of the plane.

David hit the brakes and forced the engines into full reverse, the engines screamed and he was convinced they would blow at any time sending shards of shrapnel towards them but there was nothing he could do now. He had to force them, he had to stop the plane even if it meant damaging the engines beyond repair.

The end of the clearing was approaching fast, he could see the huge trees at the edge of the forest coming up on him quickly. He pushed his feet harder onto the brake pedals, his legs almost fully-stretched, the aircraft was slowing but it wasn't going to be enough, he was going to hit the approaching trees unless he took action.

Releasing the brakes a little and easing the reverse thrust on the engines back, he turned the nose wheel round and the plane instantly responded by pitching to the right side. The whole airframe leaned to the left, he was thrown to his left, using his elbow on the side of his seat to try and stay as level as he could he forced himself back up, he had to keep control.

His empty coffee cup flew across his lap, he straightened the wheel out and he was now facing back down the clearing. He hit the brakes again and forced the engines into reverse. With a deafening roar from the engines the plane started to slow down, the vibrations became less and eventually with one last groan the plane came to a shuddering halt, the nose pitched down and then sprang back up.

He sat back in his seat and took his feet off the brake pedals. His feet ached with the pressure that he had put on them, his hand eased the throttles back and the engines slowly wound down until they fell back to a low hum. He looked around the flight deck. The usually tidy deck was littered with flight notes that been flung around during the landing, some of the over head panels had come loose due the vibrations and now they hung there held up only by the wires that connected the switches to the main loom of the aircraft.

Both pairs of headsets were lying on the floor, the co-pilot's set was smashed. They had hit the dashboard hard when the plane hit the ground and exploded; sending pieces of black plastic everywhere.

David's had fared better, the left ear cover was cracked and the mic stem was bent but they looked in working order. He undid his seat harness and followed his usual procedure of shutting down all the plane's systems that he no longer needed.

Fastening the overhead boards back into place, he finally shut the engines down. With an ever-decreasing whistling they fell silent, the huge fans that drew the air in slowed until they stopped spinning.

Half the flight deck was no longer lit and it too fell into silence. As he rested for a few seconds wiping his brow and stroking the top of the dashboard as if he was praising the plane for its landing in the same way a rider praises a horse after a difficult jump, he took off his pilot's aviator glasses he threw them onto the dashboard and rubbed his eyes, they felt sore and tired. He had had a long night by anybody's standards and now he was feeling it, his body's defences against fatigue and pain were depleted and he was now feeling both. Now the plane was down, (although he didn't know where down was) he could relax, if only for a little while.

Lynsey came in to see David sat back in his chair, his hands resting over the control column. He had heard the door open and turned around to see her entering.

"You did it, thank you, thank you."

"Only just," David replied.

Lynsey sat next to him and they both stared out of the windows.

"Do you recognise any of this, David?"

"No, nothing, the trees seem different somehow, bigger, unusual shapes; even the sky looks unusual."

Lynsey smiled. "We're not in Kansas anymore."

David smiled back at her and gently nodded.

"Do you want me to do the usual evacuation drill?" Lynsey asked.

"No, let's not open all the exits and put the chutes out until we know where we are and what has happened. Gather the passengers together and I'll come back and talk to them directly."

Lynsey nodded and headed back out to the passengers. David picked up his damaged headset and tried the radio again, but again nothing but static. There was no answer on any band or on any frequency, and what was just as strange was that none of the GPS equipment is working, every piece of technology that depended on GPS all said the same thing, "No satellite found."

He shook his head, he had heard of very rare occasions when one or even two pieces of equipment had failed, but he had never heard of all of the equipment failing, it just didn't happen in modern aircraft. He checked the damage control panel and fire controls, everything was reading a-okay, apart from the hydraulics. He knew something had happened to the system because of the shuddering and the difficulty of control just before he touched down, he knew the hydraulic systems were staring to fail. But as far as the rest of aircraft was concerned, everything was fine

David stood up and looked around the flight deck, checking one last time that everything that should be off was off. He placed his headset on its hook and headed through business class where Holly was sitting, still wincing at her injury. David walked across to her and knelt down beside her.

"Holly, how are you doing?"

"I'm in a lot of pain, David, my arm is so sore, every little movement is agony."

David placed a hand on her forehead and brushed her hair away, as he did he smiled. "Won't be long and we'll get you to a hospital." Holly just smiled as best she could, but she could see perfectly well out of the window and she knew by the view she was a long way from any hospital.

Standing up, he headed through the galley and into the economy section where the passengers had now all gathered.

"Ladies and Gentlemen, I am pleased to tell you that we have landed safely and I would ask that you remain here while myself and my crew inspect the aircraft and the immediate area outside. Thank you."

Gesturing to Lynsey, David headed back to the galley and the lift down into the hold. Taking Lynsey to one side he carefully whispered to her so that no-one could hear.

"Lynsey, once we're in the hold I'll open the cargo bay door and lower myself out through that, you stay by the door to help me back in."

"Ok, Captain." One by one they went down in to the cargo

bay. David led Lynsey through the bay making sure she didn't see Steven's body. Although it was wrapped up, it was unmistakable, and the last thing he needed now was Lynsey seeing it.

He pulled the safety catch and pushed the release for the door, it jolted and eased up into its open position. David dropped the thick black nylon net over the side and carefully lowered himself out of the aircraft and dropped onto the thick lush moss; the plane's wheels had now sunk down into.

Stepping back away from the fuselage he could see the passengers looking down out of the windows. He waved at Lynsey and held two thumbs up to gesture that he was ok. Nervously, Lynsey copied him.

He moved far enough away to take in the full length of the plane, it was then he realised what the shuddering and crashing was when he made his landing and why the hydraulics had started to fail. Looking towards the back of the plane he could see that the top section of the tail had been ripped completely off. Even if he had enough fuel for another landing attempt he would not have been able to, he would have lost control and the aircraft would have gone down.

David knew before he left the flight deck it would never fly again, but until he saw the damage to the tail he had at least held onto some small hope. But not now, now it was beyond any doubt, wherever this was; is where they would be staying until help arrived, if help arrived!

David looked back at Lynsey and then back towards the trees he had flown over just before he had touched down. He walked back towards the open cargo door and Lynsey.

"How's it looking, David?" David looked up at her and shook his head, "Not good at all, the wheels have sunk to their axles, the tail's damaged, we're about out of fuel and the hydraulics are shot, wherever we are Lynsey is where we're staying!"

Lynsey sank back the expression on her face dropped from

one of optimism to a look of defeat.

David went on, "I'm going to head over to the trees where the plane was damaged, I want to try and find the lost section of tail."

Lynsey sat back up, she seemed to snap back to attention.

"Are you sure that's a good idea, David, we don't know where we are!"

David shrugged his shoulders.

"I need to try and find it, Lynsey, when we do get rescued they'll want it so they can put together what happened."

David turned and started to walk towards the front of the aircraft and the trees they had flown over.

Lynsey watched him as far as she could until he disappeared under the fuselage.

Walking away from the plane he noticed how thick and lush the vegetation was and the heat, he had just noticed it, but God it was hot, the air seemed thick, sticky almost, the whole environment seemed surreal almost unnatural.

He removed his tie and stuffed it into his back pocket, undid the top two buttons on his shirt, and rubbed his hands around the back of his neck which was now moist with sweat.

Turning slightly he looked back at the plane. It looked strange, somehow out of scale like a model aircraft that had been left on the lawn after a child had finished playing with it. He was approaching the trees. From behind the bushes that skirted the perimeter of the forest he could see the reflection of the afternoon sun from what he assumed was a piece of metal.

"That's it," he whispered, as he turned behind the clump of bushes that were hiding the piece of aircraft and stopped dead in his tracks.

Lynsey had long lost sight of David after he had crossed under the fuselage on his way to the other side of the clearing.

The sun low in the afternoon sky was shining in to the cargo bay and bathing her in a warm and restful glow. She had hung her legs over the edge of the opening and leant back on her arms, her head raised towards the sun and her eyes closed as she enjoyed what was left of its heat before it set behind the trees that surrounded the clearing that had offered a refuge to the stricken aircraft.

She did not see or hear her attacker. In fact she was completely unaware that she was in any danger at all. The last thing she would ever remember of this life was not the sun that offered comfort and warmth, or even the aircraft that she hung her legs out of which gave her shelter, what Lynsey would remember last was the searing pain and blistering heat that suddenly came from her left leg, then the panic that set in as she was pulled from the cargo bay with such force and ferocity that she had no time at all to react.

She hit the ground hard, so hard and so unprepared her arms still hadn't managed to protect her face, her nose hit first, it shattered and instantly she was dazed, her eyes watered heavily and she could feel the blood oozing down her face and she could taste it in the back of her throat.

Coughing and gasping she scrambled to turn, to get up and flee but then came the weight, a huge weight on her back, pinning her down to the ground, making her breathing laboured and difficult, her face forced down into the long thick moss that covered the ground The pain from her leg now throbbing and radiating out to the rest of her body, she felt herself starting to shake, her heartbeat began to race, sweat streamed out of every pore in her body and she felt the warm sensation of urine as her bladder uncontrollably emptied.

She turned her eyes in their sockets as far as she could, to try and see what this was. She knew it was an animal of some kind but she had no idea what, but she could feel it, its breath, a warm putrid breath, coming in waves on the back of her head.

She tried to call out, to call for help, but all she could manage was a whimper, her mouth curled uncontrollably in the corners tears streaked down her face.

"Please, please," she repeated, she positioned her hands as if she was about to do push ups. Mustering all her remaining strength she pushed up against the weight that was holding her down, but she couldn't move, her arms collapsed beside her lying limp. Then the breathing became a growl, a low grumbling sound and she could feel the heat of breath on the back of her neck, "What was it? What was it waiting for?" The thought flashed through her mind and immediately after it had she thought nothing else. Everything for Lynsey went black and her pain vanished.

David stood in disbelief, his hands frozen by his side; his mind trying desperately to make sense of what his eyes were looking at.

There was the broken piece of tail, but under it lying dead was an animal that he had only seen in books and in B-movies when he was child, the kind of movies he would sit and watch at his grandparents on a Saturday morning with awe and wonder as the stop motion monsters reeked havoc in some small Mexican town after escaping from a side show.

He didn't know its given scientific name he didn't know much about it at all, all he knew was that what he was standing looking at was called by everybody, everywhere: a dinosaur.

After a few seconds he moved in for a closer look. Crouching down next to it, his hand touched it and then pulled back instantly then reached out again. He stroked the skin around the leg and moved onto its stomach, this was real whatever this is called it was real, dead, but real. He could clearly see where the section of tail had hit the animal crushing its skull with one violent strike. He raised himself back up, he could see that the sun was starting to set and wherever this place was, he didn't want to be out in the open if these animals are indeed wandering around freely: especially in the dark.

As he turned and headed back out into the clearing he could see the aircraft. He was looking at it now as a sanctuary and a place of safety and he started back toward it, his pace faster with every stride he took until he broke into a run. As he got closer the setting sun behind it was streaming all around the plane; almost blotting it from view in a golden - even painful - haze, he raised his arm to shield his eyes. He made it back under the fuselage and made his way to the other side where Lynsey would be sat waiting for him. He came out from underneath and turned to face the open cargo bay, but there was no sign of Lynsey. The cargo net was still hanging down but she was not there, he reached up for the net and started to climb it, as he reached the bay he hauled himself inside and turned to pull the net in, that was when he saw the blood on the ground, he hadn't seen until it now, the sun was setting and he had to be up above it to see it.

The panic set in again, "Lynsey!" he shouted. He turned to see if she was in the cargo bay but he knew deep down she wasn't, he climbed back down the net as quickly as he could.

Now, he knew something had happened, he saw blood stains on the ground that led under the plane. "This must be her blood!" he thought and it was everywhere, it was splattered on the bright chrome work of the underside of the aircraft's body, it was sprayed over the ground and even as far as the undercarriage and crucially, it was leading out towards the back of the plane and the trees that were so close by.

He saw a black high-heeled shoe, he knew this belonged to Lynsey because he had always joked with her about how uncomfortable they must have been to work in, and he knew what it meant. Instantly, fear set in and his flight response told him to run! He turned and grabbed the net. As quickly as he could he pulled himself back in to the cargo bay and pulled the net in. Facing the open door, he was convinced that at any second whatever had taken Lynsey would jump through the open door and grab him as well. The sun was setting fast and his view through the door was becoming more limited as every second passed.

From the back-lit cargo bay, he was looking into a near black void, the trees and all the unusual features he and Lynsey had commented on after the landing were gone, it was just black and it was terrifying. At last the net was in, he reached over and thumped the button that closed the door, the electric motor started to whine and instantly the door began to shut. "C'mon, c'mon," he orded the door to move quicker as it inched its way down, he was willing, pleading the door to close, pushing the button repeatedly though he knew it wouldn't make it faster but he had to try. His heart was racing, he had seen enough bad horror flicks to know that just as the door was about to close something always got in.

He was fixated on the door, the gap was becoming smaller and smaller; the darkness outside was being shut out. Eventually it clunked shut and the noisy electric motor stopped. He reached over and pulled the safety catch to its lock position. He fell back exhausted, breathing heavily; slowly he raised himself up and started back towards the lift that would take him to the passengers. When he reached the galley, he went into business class and walked over to Holly who was still lying where they had left her a short while ago.

"Holly."

"Yes, captain."

"I think you need to come in here and listen to what I have to say."

Holly pulled the blanket back and eased herself from the seat. Grimacing and wincing she followed David into the economy class. David tried as best he could to stand up straight and appear calm and in control. As he stepped through the curtains the passengers were clustered in the middle aisle.

"Ladies & Gentlemen!" he announced, he moved towards them clutching at the chair backs and leaning heavily against them.

"What's happening?" William asked.

David turned and gestured Holly to pass him and join the passengers.

David smiled, took a deep breath and rested against the back of a seat. He crossed his legs and arms and smiled at the passengers.

"Ladies & Gentlemen!" he repeated, "You have no doubt noticed that where we have landed is not where we're supposed to be. The truth of the matter is..." he paused..."I don't know where we are or possibly when we are."

"When we are?" Holly replied.

"Look, what I'm about to tell you sounds ridiculous and stupid, but you need to listen!"

David went on to explain what he had found when he went looking for the detached piece of plane, he made it clear that with the lack of fuel and damage to the tail as well as the fact that the wheels had now sunk into the soft moss; the plane could not take off again, so wherever they were was where they were staying. Then he paused, his face changed, a look of sadness came across it, his eyes started to water and they looked heavy and mournful, the colour washed away from him. He looked like someone who was about to deliver bad news, and he was! Looking around the group of people he explained that Steven had been killed during the event and that something had happened to Lynsey, and whilst he didn't know what, at first light he had decided he was going to find out.

William stepped forward. "So what do we do?" David's stance and expression changed, his colour came back and he wiped his face clear of the few tears that had escaped his eyes. Now he looked like the captain again, a man in charge that knew what to do and everybody felt comforted and calmer for it.

"Ok, the plane can provide power for now but to get the most we can from the generators we need to cut the power usage. We should switch off everything we're not using, all the overhead lights throughout the cabins that we don't need and the screens. As for everything else I'll go into avionics and shut down all the unnecessary systems. We should also keep all the cabin doors closed tight, and use the cargo bay door to get in and out of the plane. We can split into teams and go through the cargo there might be things that we can use."

David sighed and dropped his head. Slowly he looked back up at the group, the mournful look had come back again, but it was different, he had a determined look about him as well, this time it wasn't just grief it was also anger and this time he managed to keep his eyes clear. "Tomorrow I'm heading out to find out what happened to Lynsey, any help would be appreciated, and we need to bury Steven"

One by one the cabin lights on the aircraft started to blink out, and the sound of the air flowing through the ventilation system disappeared, there seemed no point in keeping it running now they were stuck fast on the ground.

The LCD screens blinked and row by row went blank, the back-lit switches above the seats that would summon a steward or adjust the air flow went dim as did the floor lighting.

David was in the avionics bay shutting down all the systems that they no longer needed. The exit and fasten seat belt signs became dark and finally the soft blue illumination that back-lit the overhead lockers and bathed the entire cabin in a soft calming glow was switched off.

The aircraft was slowly plunged into darkness, its bright silhouette against the now dark trees slowly disappeared, until only a few lights remained on where the group were huddled together.

David made his way back to the flight deck and sat in the

captain's chair looking directly ahead. The ultra-bright landing lights now lit the pitch black outside the aircraft and the ground caught in the beam stood out a brilliant green against the void around them. All the other outside lights used for navigation and recognition on the wings, fuselage and tail had been extinguished. David put his hand on the switch and with a flick of his finger outside went deathly black. The flight deck was now only dimly lit, the few remaining readouts and instruments that could not be switched off without cutting all of the plane's power gave off a soft green glow, and the one white light above him hardly competed with it. His hand moved above his head and it too was put out.

William sat in his seat and looked out the window into the pitch black. Turning round he watched the other passengers settling down and talking amongst themselves, some of them headed through to business class to use the fold down beds. He smiled to himself and thought, "Some people will use any excuse for a free upgrade."

Sarah was across the other side of the plane talking to a worried looking women, she had her hands in the women's hands which were clasped tight on her knees. Sarah caught his eye and smiled at him. William nodded and gave a quick smile before turning his gaze back to the window. Reaching up he pulled down the blind and fell into a restless and unsettled sleep.

He awoke to sounds of movement. Some of the passengers were making a start on the day, using the toilets and galley. It amazed him how they seemed to be sticking to their normal routines, sitting having breakfast from the food that remained in the galley, reading yesterday's papers again, smiling to himself he turned and lifted the blind. He was met with a leaden grey sky, rain streaked against his small window and the plane softly and only just noticeably, sawed as the wind that ran across the clearing caught the wings and lifted the huge frame. He pulled his blanket back across him and stood up. He figured he might as well join in and have breakfast while there was some food left. David had slept in the pilot's bunk which was located behind the flight deck. Making his way to the galley he stopped by Holly to see how she was. He stooped down beside her and before he spoke he looked at her just for a moment. She was lying in a foetal position, with a blanket over her, she looked rested and comfortable; her head buried deep into one of the complimentary pillows offered only to the highest paying customers.

She opened her eyes and immediately she smiled at him.

"How are you doing?"

"Ok, the pain seems to be either going or I'm getting used to it" she replied in a soft sleepy voice, "but I think we're running out of painkillers."

"I have some in my overnight bag, Holly, I'm sure everything will be ok sooner or later."

David didn't believe the words coming out of his mouth, he had no reason to think that it would be ok or that they would ever be found or helped in any way. He didn't add anything else to their conversation, he just stood and turned towards the galley.

After everybody had eaten and done whatever their normal morning start-up ritual was he gathered them all by the curtains that separated the galley and passenger cabins. "Ok, I need volunteers. I need people to go through the luggage to see if anything can be used either now or later. I need someone to stay with Holly and I need someone to come with me."

William looked around, and no-one spoke, they all seemed too nervous to be the first. They reminded him of an audience that had gone to see a magician who had then asked for a volunteer he wanted to humiliate on stage. He stepped forward, "Hi, I'm William." He extended his arm towards

David.

"David," was the only reply as he took William's hand and gave it a strong clenching shake.

"I'll come with you, David."

"Thanks."

David let go of his hand and smiled at him. Sarah looked up from the floor that she had been staring at like a child in a class who desperately didn't want to be picked on by the teacher to read or explain whatever the subject matter was.

"I'm Sarah. I've done some work at my local health clinic, I'll look after Holly."

David nodded and gestured for Sarah to go past him to where Holly was.

"Hi, I'm Nicholas, but please, call me Nick."

David turned to his left from where the voice was coming. The man was about 5ft 10", 180lbs, he was bald with a small goatee beard and one earring in his right ear. He was wearing a plain pair of jeans and white plain T-shirt with brown suede shoes. "As far as the luggage is concerned, why don't we just go through our own and take out what we know we can use?"

David had a look that was a cross of frustration and agreement running across his face. "That's fine, Nick," he answered, "but we don't just carry passengers' luggage, we also have luggage that didn't make the other flights and was left behind and we also courier stuff as well, so there will be things down there that none of you will be aware of."

Nick stepped back into the small crowd as if to acknowledge the fact that his idea was not a very good one.

"Ok," David broke the uneasy silence that had followed Nick's idea, "The rest of you follow me down to the cargo bay, the actual passenger luggage is always located on the left of the aircraft, so you all know what's in there. The stuff you need to go through will be on the right side, any questions?" As always with these situations, there were none.

He led the passengers down into the cargo bay through the hatch. Now the power was only feeding essential systems the lift had been made redundant. Once down he took them to the cargo bay door that he had scrambled through the previous night after finding traces of blood from where Lynsey had waited for him.

"This is the cargo bay door, and I think this is where Lynsey was taken from. Once William and I are out I want you to close the door behind us."

Another member of the group stepped forward, "Hi, ermm how will we know when to open it?"

David rolled his bottom lip.

"You are?"

"Oh, sorry I'm Amy."

"Ok Amy, we don't carry walkie talkies on planes and I think we can count cell phones out, so when we reach the door we'll tap three times then two, ok?"

The group nodded and accepted what they were told.

"Now, usually the door opens electronically but of course the power feeding it has been cut, so you'll have to use the manual winder here."

David pointed to what looked like a starting handle from a 1920s car, "But first remove the safety catch, then it's clockwise to open and anti-clockwise to close, and make sure once it's closed the safety catch is fastened!"

David turned to face the group.

"Behind that bulk head is Steven's body. It is wrapped but it needs to be buried, whoever does it you do it in teams and you bury him deep, and most importantly you keep a look out." With that he pushed the catch across and started to wind open the door. At first he only opened it just enough to look through as if to make sure the coast was clear, even though he didn't know what it was supposed to be clear of.

As the door opened the wind that had been gently rocking the aircraft came into the bay. Although it had died down a lot and the rain had long since stopped it still had a chill about it, the air once again seemed to feel as if it was somehow concentrated, the net started to flap and the paper labels on the cargo rustled.

When David was satisfied he turned the handle until it was far enough open for him and William to drop out the net and climb down. He tossed out the net and gestured to William to climb down with him. They crouched onto their hands and knees and lowered themselves backwards onto the net. Slowly they made their way down the net until they felt the firm ground beneath their feet. Looking back up, David gestured to Nick and watched as he pulled up the net. Once in, the door shuddered and slowly it closed sealing them both out of the safety that the plane promised. David stood under the plane looking at the ground and then up at the underside.

The blood he had seen the previous night was still there, even with the wind and rain that had pelted them overnight; it still hadn't washed it all off.

William walked over to join him. David turned. "Ready?" William simply gave him a nod and the two men set off in the direction the trail of blood led them.

Chapter Four

Four weeks had passed since Bruce and Simon had arrived and been met by the sight that would change their lives forever. They had worked feverishly to try and work out what they had found and the aircraft was now completely unearthed, though they had still not gained access to it.

Bruce was at site bravo with Andrea. Since their difficult start they had formed a working relationship that was workable, even if it was a delicate one, it was based on mutual respect for each other. It was painfully obvious to anyone who had worked with either of them that they both knew their jobs well, and that at least they had that in common. Site alpha had been abandoned, apart from the initial find, nothing new had been discovered there and the team was now permanently working on site charlie under the guidance of Simon.

Bruce and Andrea were standing at the foot of the examination table. Lying on it was the last skeleton that had been removed from the grave. The skeleton that they looked at now was male, average height and it seemed by the stress and wear and tear on the joints; he had been of average build and weight too.

After a short - and as usual direct conversation between Andrea and Bruce - they had decided to send it to the pathology lab that the other two had been sent to, to try and establish his age, how long he had been dead and if possible: the actual cause of death.

Bruce turned and headed for the exit, his next stop would be site charlie; this is where his expertise lay and if he was honest - his interest.

He stepped out of the tent and into the hot afternoon. Starting on his walk he was interrupted by Susan who had just returned from a two-day trip to the Smithsonian in Washington. She had gone following a call she had received from them.

After the first two skeletons had been examined their skulls had been carefully removed and sent there for forensic facial reconstruction, and Susan had had the call she was waiting for, they had completed them both.

"Bruce!" she yelled, as clearly as she could, but after running from her parked truck through the midday heat to find him, she was out of breath.

Bruce turned to see her running over to him.

"Susan, you're back, how did it go?"

Susan's pace slowed as she approached him. Bending forward to rest her hands on her knees, she fought to catch her breath, looking up at him she gasped out as clearly as she could, "You gotta come see this." She looked full of excitement and enthusiasm. "Really," she repeated, "you gotta come see this!"

Standing erect again she put her hands on her hips and smiled at him. Breathing a little easier now she led Bruce over to her truck and flung open the tailgate. Inside was a large wooden box, the type that would house an antique sewing machine or other valuables; it was highly polished and had brass fasteners at the bottom and a leather handle on the top.

"Here, help me carry this over to my tent, I don't want anybody else to see it, not yet."

Bruce simply shrugged his shoulders and leaned into the truck, grabbing one side of the box. They walked carefully inside, stepping to Susan's tent and placed it onto a picnic table.

"Ok, what's in the mystery box, Susan?"

She smiled and unclipped the bottom fasteners. Slowly she raised the lid of the box leaving only the bottom of it on the table. As she did Bruce could see what the excitement was, in front of him looking directly back at him were the reconstructed faces of *John & Jane Doe*.

Susan placed the lid on the floor and looked at Bruce.

"So, what do you think?"

"This is them?" he replied.

"Well, as close as they think, they can't tell how much fat was on the face or hair colour, but they can interpret skeletal features that reveal the age, sex, ancestry, and anatomical features like: facial asymmetry, evidence of injuries before death, etc."

Bruce looked up at Susan, "I've seen this kind of thing on the Discovery Channel but never up close."

Turning back to the female. "So, the blonde hair is a guess?"

"They say it is, Bruce, but it's an educated guess; the same as the lip shapes and eye colour etc."

"So why blonde, Susan? Why not brunette or red?"

Susan looked a little disappointed; the excitement now removed from her face. She should have expected it from Bruce; he was very matter of fact; very much for what could be proven.

"Bruce, I don't know, I didn't question them. I accepted what they said, but at least now we have some idea of who they were, and there's no reason why we can't investigate further to try and ID them."

Bruce turned to her and sighed, even he could tell that he had overstepped the mark, he had taken the wonderment out of it for her, like his grandmother had one Saturday morning while he watched his B-movies in wonder, she had explained to him how the dinosaurs he was watching were just clay models; no larger than the toys he would play with after the movie. He knew from this exactly how she felt.

"Susan what you have here is really very good, and of course you're right, this is a big step forward."

With that he felt reprieved, coming from Bruce that was as much as anybody could expect and as close to giving a compliment as he did and he got the reaction he hoped for.

"Thanks, Bruce, from a cynical old sod like you that means a lot, but I think we should keep it quiet just for now."

Bruce agreed with her. "I think you're right, the last thing we need is pictures of these two splashed over the internet! I'm going over to see Simon, you coming?"

"Give me a minute, Bruce." Susan replaced the lid and they restarted Bruce's journey to site Charlie.

The walk over was a quiet one. Neither Bruce nor Susan broke the silence. After giving a verbal pat on the back, Bruce wasn't really sure he had much else to say to her and Susan didn't want to spoil the moment. They stepped into the hangar. Instantly they were out of the sun's relentless gaze and bathed in the orange glow that they had become accustomed to. Bruce wiped the sweat from his head with his forearm and headed through the air-conditioned environment towards the aircraft.

As he did, he could see Simon standing on the wing, closest to them. He had grown in confidence since this whole thing had started and the awe and respect Simon once so eagerly showed Bruce had slipped away.

Bruce didn't mind this, at least now he didn't follow him around like a lost puppy that continually brought him presents to show his loyalty.

"Hi, Simon."

Simon turned, "Hi, Boss."

Bruce smiled a little, at least he still called him that.

"Hi, Susan, how did the Smithsonian go?"

Susan looked at Bruce, mindful of the conversation she had just had with him.

"Ok, Simon, but more importantly, how are things going here?"

Bruce and Susan looked at each other and smiled like two people who were planning a practical joke on some unsuspecting victim.

"Well, we're under the aircraft now, we have completely

unearthed it, we have jacks under it to take the weight. We don't know what condition the landing gear is in or how strong it is."

"What about the metallurgy samples they took?" Bruce, as usual, was direct with his questioning.

"Should have those back in a couple of days."

He looked at Bruce and Susan, his eye's widened, and just for a second Bruce could see that lost look of wonderment in his eyes again.

"Wanna see under it?"

Simon led them down the side of the dig under the airframe. More orange lights had been placed under the fuselage and even though it had dulled over time; what was left of the chrome finish reflected some of the light and bathed the whole area and against the colour of the desert floor: this was an eerie place to be.

"We think the best way in is through the main cargo bay door. There are signs of wear and tear down the side of the fuselage and we think this is where they got in and out of it when they….."

Simon stopped and Bruce turned towards him, "When they what, Simon?"

"When they, well we think they must have lived on it for a while."

Susan walked under the plane towards the rear. She took out her trusted soft bristle brush that any good palaeontologist carries with them and started to gently dust the bottom of the fuselage near the cargo bay door.

Bruce watched her and he saw her face change, her expression changed from inquisitive to curious and then to shock. Turning her head to Bruce she gestured for them both to come over, pointing up at the fuselage directly above them they could see the dark splattered stains that they all knew was dried blood.

"Guys, this is what I think it is, right?"

"Looks like it, Susan," came a heavy response from Simon, his words laboured.

They could see the pattern the blood made where it was still visible. She knew enough about forensics and strike patterns to know that what was left under here represented a violent event.

Simon rubbed the blood marks with the tips of his fingers.

"Should we enter this at all, Bruce?"

Bruce turned to him, "Why wouldn't we?"

"It could be a tomb, you know, it's like the whole Titanic argument; some people say it shouldn't be disturbed."

"Really, Simon," Bruce's reply snapped out, "but, unlike the Titanic, we have no idea why this plane is here and if by some miracle the black box is retrievable; we might find out."

Simon knew he was defeated and decided to back down, besides Bruce was in charge so whatever his thoughts were on the matter they would have no bearing on the outcome and in the end he knew they would go in.

Susan brought their attention back to the blood on the fuselage. "If we get a sample off this, you know we might just be able to find out who it belonged to!"

Bruce nodded and turned his attention back to Simon, "When can we get the door open?"

Simon drew his breath as if to indicate he was pondering and he needed a little moment to find an answer. "Well, we'll need cutting gear and some kind of a support to hold the door once it's removed."

"Ok," replied Bruce, but Simon knew as the word came out of his mouth his reply wasn't finished.

"Ok, that's what you need, what I asked is when?"

"12-hours, Bruce, I'll have you in."

Bruce and Susan turned and started to make their way up the side of the dig. They came out at the front of the plane directly opposite the flight deck windows. Bruce squinted and looked as hard as he could at the glass, but it was dirty, thick with eons of dust and rain and just for now the plane was holding onto its secrets.

Bruce returned to his tent, closing the flap behind him and made his way to his field workstation. Sitting at the desk he opened the lid of his laptop, this was the part he didn't care for, reporting in on his progress and dealing with the clones that made up the chain of command; most of whom he was convinced had no field experience and had ended up being his manager because of some piece of paper that declared beyond doubt they had the aptitude and ability to do the job.

After what seemed like an eternity, Bruce finished his reports and moved himself over to his bunk. He set the alarm on his phone and lay back. The sun was still hanging in the sky and his tent was impossibly bright and humid but he was determined to get some sleep; he hadn't much since arriving and it was starting to take its toll. He was feeling tired and fatigued; his temper was shorter than normal, even though he promised himself a while ago he would try his hardest to arrest it. He knew how to manage people and he knew that continuous shouting and growling at them wasn't the way to do it.

Simon stood a few feet away from the frame of the door as the cutting crew worked on it. The brace they had put in place to hold the door stood firmly against the wall of the dig and the desert floor under the plane. The cutters were nearly all the way round the frame of the door. He stood almost trembling with the anticipation of what secrets would be revealed once they got inside. With a shudder the door dropped a few centimetres as the cutters met midway on the top side, the brace now held fast, taking the full weight of the reinforced air-tight door. The crew Simon had hired knew nothing of what they were working on, after Bruce's strict privacy and media blackout rules that had been stringently imposed since they first glanced at the tail section he knew it had to stay this way.

He was desperate to lower the brace down but he had to clear the hangar of all non-essential staff and he must, without fail, get Bruce and Susan. Simon started for Susan's and Bruce's tents, leaving the hangar.

The sun was suspended low in the evening sky, the paradox of this place was the heat in the day and the sheer cold of the night. They had already turned the air conditioning off in the hangar to allow it to capture the last heat the day offered that would keep it comfortable during the night. He reached Bruce's tent first and opened the flap. Bruce was already pulling his pants on, woken by his alarm a few minutes earlier.

He had eagerly got up knowing that the deadline for Simon was almost up and the door would soon be off.

"Simon, come on in, don't be shy." Bruce seemed in a better mood than the last time they had had a conversation.

Simon smiled and continued in. "Well?" "The door is open," Simon replied, he went on, "the brace is holding it shut for now, I wanted to clear the hangar first."

Bruce seemed pleased and he was.

"Excellent work, Simon, ok, let's go get Susan, I know she's as excited as I am."

The two men left Simon's tent. The sun had now almost disappeared, the generators had kicked in and the entire site now worked to the sound of diesel engines as they supplied the electricity to power the huge halogen lights that now floodlit the whole area. Even with these lights it was tricky going, the shadows cast by rocks and changing shape of the desert floor changed continuously making every step not much more than a guess.

After a short walk they reached Susan's tent, but this time Simon didn't walk straight in; instead they shook the canvas flap and called her name. Instantly she replied, "Ok, Simon, I'm coming out." After a few seconds she emerged holding a powerful hand light. Looking at the two escorts that had arrived she smiled. "Hi, boys," as usual she was cheerful. Bruce couldn't help but think that she played it up around him just to wind him up a little. "Let's go see what we have."

The three of them made their way through the night towards the hangar. The large blue tent now seemed to glow a strange mixture of the blue fabric and orange lights that lit the interior, the unnatural radiance that resulted glowed in the pitch black of the night. Reaching the hangar they entered and made their way to the aircraft that now sat waiting for them, ready to reveal whatever strange events had put it there. The walk over from Susan's tent had been a quiet one, even with her quips the response she had received from both Bruce and Simon had sent a very clear message to her that neither of them had the mind to continue with her jovial manner, this along with the always strange and surreal night time walk had left them all somewhat sombre.

The three of them made their way down into the dig under the aircraft. The brace was a fairly simple piece of equipment, it was essentially a large and immensely strong metal frame that allowed the operator to lower the support frame up or down by a mechanical winding system.

Simon took hold of the handle that operated it and began rotating it. The door shuddered just as it had all those years before when the passengers and crew had made their way in and out of the plane. As the seals split there was a rush of hissing air and the air that had been trapped for 65 million years rushed out, even from the distance they stood, the pungent smell caught them. All of them without exception retreated at the stench that met them. Simon looked at Bruce and Susan and took hold of the handle again. With a judder the door continued down away from the frame of the aircraft. Eventually the brace had lowered the door as far as it could. Simon attached the ladders he had placed nearby to the lip of the open door frame and shook them to make sure they were secured. He stepped back and gestured to Bruce as if to say, *"You first."*

Bruce smiled, a thought flashed through his mind that Simon had done that out of either respect for him as his boss, or because he was just too damn scared to go in first. "I think we should allow the air pressure and quality to equalize first Simon, give it ten-minutes then we'll go through zone by zone.

Bruce and Simon had already zoned the interior of the plane off using plans they had on all the major commercial aircraft that had been produced over the last thirty-years.

Zone one would be the mid-to-forward cargo bay, this is where the door they had removed would lead them first. Zone two would be the mid-to-rear cargo bay. Zone three, the business class and flight decks; including the captain's bunk and finally zone four, economy class and back to the rear of the aircraft.

After the allotted ten-minutes, Bruce grabbed the first ladder rung and started the climb into the cargo bay. He was followed by Simon and then Susan. Bruce reached the top of the ladder and stepped into the hull. Switching on his maglite he shone it around the cargo bay, another light illuminated the bay as Simon joined him and then Susan. The bay lit up in patches forming shadows through the girder trusses that supported the floor of the passenger compartment. The shadows stretched and changed shape as they moved the lights around. The bay looked intact, in fact to Bruce he felt cheated, there was nothing at all that was unremarkable about it except the fact that all the luggage had been opened and he guessed by the lack of it that most of it had been taken or used by whoever had survived this and had used all the resources the plane had to offer them. Large luggage drums that had been cut in two were stacked by the door, Simon commented on the possibility that they could have been used for collecting fresh water.

Bruce agreed with him and started to move towards zone two. Susan stayed in zone one. She carefully moved the luggage around; disturbing it for the first time in an eon, the thick dust that had collected on it floated slowly down to the floor, dancing in the beams of the bright white light that now flooded the cargo bay. Simon knelt down next to the cargo net, he decided that they must have used it to lower themselves down and climb back up. He picked up a corner of the net and stood up. Reaching up as far as he could he extended the net, "Bruce, look at this!" Bruce turned, he could see that the net was slashed and ripped; it looked as though someone had taken a sharp carving knife to it and thrashed it in a frenzied manner.

Bruce took in a deep breath and slowly released it. Susan came and joined Simon and took hold of the other corner. Walking back away from him she stretched the net out, "Jesus," she said, "this thing looks like it's been torn to shit!"

Simon nodded, "But by what, Susan? this is a nylon net, it's made to be strong and tear-resistant; it's meant to hold big weights in flight through even the worst turbulence."

Susan looked back at the net and then to Simon, "There is only one animal that would fit the evidence we have about how long this has been down here and it is..." She stopped.

"Is what, Susan?" Bruce bellowed from further down the cargo bay.

She looked back at the net and continued, "It would be a Velocirapter. It had a huge and very sharp claw on its feet; we believe it used it for tearing at its prey to bring it down and then cut it open. Bearing in mind how thick the skin of some if its prey would have been, this net wouldn't be much of a challenge."

Bruce shook his head and looked down to the floor.

"What is it?" Susan asked. "I still can't get used to this and we've been here three weeks or so," Susan answered with an unusually sharp tone, one that snapped Bruce back to attention and brought his gaze from the floor to her.

"Well get used to it, Bruce, it's the only thing we have to work with, you've seen the fossil with the tail section that we know came from this plane and you've seen the fossilised remains of John & Jane Doe at site bravo, we need to disband the disbelief and just deal with it!"

Simon looked at Bruce, he had never heard anybody talk to Bruce like that and he had never heard Susan talk like that to anybody, but Bruce reacted well and thankfully so.

As far as Simon was concerned, the last thing he wanted to be in the middle of, right at this moment, was a pissing competition between Bruce and Susan.

"Besides," she continued, "if Raptors did attack this net because they knew people were on this plane I only hope they didn't get in!"

Bruce turned and continued towards the back of the cargo bay, as with the zone one there was nothing unusual about it other than the fact it was here to start with. He turned back and approached Susan. "Look, we can let your team inch their way over this section later, we need to go up, I need to get to avionics, that's where the black box is." "Ok, Bruce, after you," she replied. Simon let go of the remaining corner of the net and it fell heavily back to the floor, plumes of ancient dust rose from the floor and spread across covering the area around their feet, the particles of dust streamed through the intense white light of their LED torches.

They reached the short ladder that would take them up to the passenger compartment. Following Bruce, Simon and Susan raised themselves out of the hatch opening in the galley. Bruce helped Susan up and shone his maglite around. Simon and Susan did the same as they had in the cargo bay. The powerful lights streamed around the galley, illuminating it in circular patterns. The air seemed thicker up in the passenger compartment; it had a damp, almost putrid smell about it. It seemed warm and heavy and dust plumes floated through the air, highlighted by the bright torches. Simon raised the back of his right hand to his nose. "This smells awful!" Bruce raised an eyebrow and turned back towards the galley. They opened the cupboard doors and drawers. Everything was where they had expected it to be. Apart from the lack of cups and other kitchen cutlery there was nothing that struck them as bizarre.

Bruce pushed the door release on the microwave oven, it clunked and thick dust that had collected over time fell from the face of the door as it swung open, inside it was clean and dust-free, the air-tight seals around the door had held the years of dust out. Apart from the absence of the courtesy light, inside the oven looked much like his did at home.

Bruce turned to Susan, "How do you explain, why after all this time, the condition is so good? surely it should be all dust now."

Susan could offer no answer; not now, not right at this moment, she simply shrugged her shoulders and shook her head.

Simon pulled the curtain back that led into the economy class compartment. More flakes of dust and dirt danced and floated down to the floor through his light. "Bruce, I'm going into zone four." "Ok, Simon." His torch shone a stream of white light through the compartment like a warship's searchlight; shadows formed as the light was blocked by the headrest on the seats that housed the blank LCD screens. He shone it up towards the overhead cupboards. The ceiling had traces of mould on it, but nothing he hadn't seen on an aircraft that had simply just been left standing outside for ten-years or so. All the window blinds were down as they had noticed when they first unearthed it, there was no mess, nothing was out of place.

"Bruce."

"Yes, Simon," "putting aside the fact that it has survived down here, surely if the passengers and crew had had to live in here there would be some mess, some signs of usage: plates, cups, anything, but there's nothing, nothing at all!"

"I don't know what to tell you, Simon, I don't have an answer for you."

Bruce turned to Susan, "I'm heading towards the flight deck to avionics, you coming?" Susan smiled and nodded and turned to follow Bruce.

The curtain to business class and the front of the aircraft was already over at one side, their torches flooded the front compartment area and Bruce stopped abruptly. He reached out an open hand and grabbed Susan's wrist as she closed in behind him stopping her dead in her tracks. With his torch he gestured to her to follow its beam and she did, looking up slowly from the floor and her own stream of light she followed Bruce's through the dark thick still air, and it was what was at the end of the light beam that Bruce had stopped, for a chill ran down her spine and her heart started to thump inside her chest. She could feel a cold sweat running down her back as she stared ahead. There in the gloom of the barely-lit cabin - illuminated only by a single shaft of light - was the back of a man's head. Bruce let go of Susan's wrist and moved slowly towards the anonymous sullen figure that faced away from them. Susan followed closely behind him. Bruce detoured through the centre row of the business class seats and ended up opposite the figure on the other side of the cabin. The man was lying down, almost flat on a reclined seat, a plastic tumbler sat next to him, placed neatly in the holder provided. He had a blanket pulled half way up his body and they could see he was wearing a plain dark T-shirt. He had some stubble around his chin and his hair was short and ragged and had obviously been cut by him using a blunt instrument of some kind, it was tangled and rough. Susan thought about how it resembled the recreations and depictions of Stone Age man. His right hand was under the blanket, but in his left hand was a book. "Looks like he was reading when the end came," Bruce whispered in a soft voice. The man's head was buried deep in the two pillows he had rested it on.

What struck them both, the most profound thing, was the condition of the body. Unlike the other bodies in the grave that had first decomposed to skeletons and then transformed to fossils; this body hadn't. It was in a state of advanced decomposition but whatever had kept this aircraft in its condition had had the same effect on the dead body before them. Bruce rested a heavy hand on Susan's left shoulder, she turned to face him. Shining the light in her general direction so that she wasn't blinded by it, he could see the sad expression on her face, she looked sad for this man, this stranger that seemed to have died in such a peaceful way amongst the strangest of circumstance.

Bruce moved forward to the flight deck with Susan in tow. He reached the door and pushed it open. The door didn't put up a fight, it seemed eager to let him in, it was almost as if it couldn't hold on to its secrets any longer and it was relieved to be able to share them. The flight deck was bathed in the eerie orange glow that was outside in the tent, it flooded through the dirty windows that had prohibited him from seeing in this morning.

On the co-pilot's seat was a broken headset, at some point they had been smashed to pieces and had landed there. On the pilot's side the headset sat neatly in its holder, he noticed the mic arm was bent and the left ear-piece smashed. He moved the light around further and saw the shape of aviator glasses resting on the top of the dashboard, a thick layer of dust covered everything, every switch was in the exact position it should be following a controlled landing and this confirmed in Bruce's mind - beyond any doubt - his theory that the plane had been landed and it had not simply crashed. He moved his torch from the dashboard to the floor of the flight deck and the hatch that lead to avionics.

Susan followed his lead and moved the beam of her torch to the hatch. Bruce wafted at the thick layer of dust that covered the hatch locks and unclipped them, removing them he climbed down into the bay. Susan leant over the open hatchway, passing him his torch and shining hers down to give him as much light as they had available.

Bruce went to where he knew the black box would be; the two red boxes that are commonly known as one black box were there, he unlocked the catches that held them in place and one by one he passed them up to Susan. Once up he looked around avionics, and as with the flight deck what struck him was that the controls, in fact everything, was as it should have been, all the systems they wouldn't have needed once down had been disabled; only the most crucial systems had been allowed to stay on.

Bruce started to feel a chill, he understood now what Simon had meant when he had compared it to the Titanic. This plane really did feel like a tomb. By the time Bruce was normally involved in aircraft incidents little else remained apart from fragments, broken parts laid, even strewed across sometimes large areas after the aircraft had impacted against the ground and exploded. But not this time, this time the pilot had managed to land the plane and now with the body in business class and the condition of it, it was starting to feel as though he was trespassing and now he had the black box he needed, he wanted to leave it and never come back, but even as that wish filled his mind, he knew that at some point he would have to.

He climbed out of the opening and replaced the hatch cover. Picking up the red cases that held the data drives, he left the flight deck with Susan and closed the door behind them.

As they entered business class again they saw Simon standing over the body. He saw their light dancing and flickering around the cabin as they walked through it and he turned towards them, "Did you find them, Bruce?" His voice was grave and it had a low pitch to it, it was as if he was conducting the funeral service for this mystery passenger they had found and felt he needed to talk with a sombre respectful tone.

Bruce didn't comment on it, he understood, in fact he found himself speaking the same, "I did, Simon, let's get out." They climbed down the ladder back into the cargo bay. Bruce ensured he was last to leave, half-way down the ladder when his head still remained above the galley floor, he shone his torch round for one last look, feeling sad for the people who had been on the flight he pulled the hatch cover back on and with the lowering of his torch it fell back into darkness.

The forensic team had already started to unload the cargo bay, huge powerful halogen lights now flooded every part and hidden corner. Box by box they were passing each piece of the remaining luggage and belongings out, stacking it carefully, numbering it so that it could be checked at a microscopic level for anything that might identify what this plane was doing here.

Bruce, Simon and Susan climbed out of the cargo bay back into the hangar. As they started up the side of the dig back towards the exit, Bruce stopped and turned to Susan, "We need to get the body out of there, we need to find out who he is, how he died, and when."

Susan agreed.

"The forensic team are working on the zoned areas one and

two for now, but I'll instruct them in the morning on our mystery man, but for now I need to go to bed, I need to sleep."

Bruce nodded, "Ok, Susan, I'll leave it with you."

Heading out of the hangar into the night again, the fresh desert air seemed to clear any dust and dirt that had got onto them from the interior on the plane. Bruce reached his tent and placed the two metal containers on the floor, he would examine them in the morning. He hadn't said anything to Susan when she had admitted defeat and the need to go to bed, but he had felt the same, he knew he was done for the day, he had nothing else to give and saw no reason to push on, besides the feeling of exhaustion he had felt this morning had been amplified a thousand times over by what he had seen and felt tonight. Tonight he would sleep and as he lay down and pulled his blankets over him he would find out that it would be a troubled and disturbing sleep.

The following morning Bruce woke up to another blazing hot day. It was only 7:42am by the red glowing dials on his bedside clock but already he was sweating heavily and he could feel the dryness in the back of his throat. He turned over and reached for the bottle of water he had constantly kept by his bedside since they had arrived. Taking a few sips then wiping the odd drip from his lips he lay back flat on his bed. He stared for a while at the yellow canvas roof above him before making the effort to get up and go to the shower block.

Susan had not had a good night's sleep. She reached her tent physically and emotionally drained from what they had found and the feeling she had got from walking around the interior of the aircraft. She had felt like a tomb raider, as though she should not have been there. She was trespassing on that which is most sacred and holy, a person's final resting place.

She kicked the sheet off that was covering her with her feet and sat on the edge of the bed trying to put the pieces together; she knew there had to be an answer; there was always an answer but what the hell this one was she wasn't sure if they would ever know.

She looked over at her clock it was old fashioned wind-up alarm clock with two large bells on each side of the round face, scratched and dusty. The once bright red paint that covered the metal body was faded and dull after spending so much time in the sun on so many different expeditions.

Reaching over she picked the clock up and felt for the winder on the back giving it a turn. She smiled as she remembered the day she was given it as present, her father had bought it as a last-minute gift. She had rung him when she had been given her first placement on a dig site in the Bad Lands. Of all the gifts she had received from friends and family for her first expedition this was the only one that remained, it had seemed a strange gift at the time and she remembered her mother denouncing the gift as, "Typical of that man, no thought for anything or anyone; no wonder I left him!" But Susan loved it and took it everywhere with her; especially now as her father was dead.

She leaned across and placed it carefully on the table next to her bed. She stood up and slipped out of her pyjama bottoms. Peeling her T-shirt off she felt the warmth of the sun on her body and a slight breeze blowing through the vent flaps of the tent. She washed and pulled on a clean set of field clothes, which mainly consisted of a clean dark T-shirt a pair of comfortable knickers, combat style shorts and thick socks that she wore under her heavy black boots.

She had made two promises to her father before he had died, that she would wind her clock up every morning and that she would wear thick socks and boots so she couldn't be stung or bitten by anything in the desert and she had kept to them religiously. She tied her hair back in a pony tail and stepped out in to the day. The sun was already high in the sky which as usual was a deep blue and completely unspoilt by any wandering clouds. She closed the flap, fastening it, and headed over to the field kitchen where she saw Bruce sitting having his morning coffee. He looked much as she did; un-rested and tired.

"Morning, Bruce."

He looked up, he didn't need to see who it was, he could recognise Susan's voice now.

She sat opposite him with a mug of coffee and a slice of toast.

"Morning, Susan, how did you sleep?"

"Not well, Bruce, I don't think I dreamed much but if I did I certainly can't remember it."

Bruce clenched his jaw, "Same here, if I got two hours last night I did well."

"So, what do you think we should do first, Bruce?"

He placed his coffee down on the table and held onto the mug with both hands. Taking a deep breath he looked around the kitchen like someone ready to tell a secret and checking for anybody that was listening to them. "I think we need to get Andrea and her team to remove our mystery man. I think we need to do that delicately; we don't need everyone to know about him. We'll get her to take him straight to bravo, she might be able to give us what we need for now."

Susan sat back in her chair and put the now empty mug and plate on the table in front of her. "I'll go see Andrea and get her over to charlie, her team can handle our man from there, she has the experience and know how."

Bruce took another sip, his hands still grasping the cup tightly, "I'll see you over at bravo in a couple of hours. I need to check-in with Simon and I need to start downloading the information from the boxes I got last night."

Susan stood and left Bruce to his coffee. She pulled her sunglasses down from her forehead to block some of the sun's glare out as she made her way to site bravo.

Entering the huge tent she made her way over to Andrea's makeshift office.

"Hi, Susan," she turned to see Andrea following in behind her.

"You're an early bird this morning, to what pleasure do I owe for this visit?"

Susan smiled and gestured Andrea to follow her to the office. Once they were both inside Susan closed the door, leaving one hand on the handle she turned to face Andrea.

"We entered the aircraft last night and it gave us more questions than answers. Apart from the condition of the thing and the fact that Bruce is now convinced beyond doubt that whoever they were lived on it after it landed, we found something."

Susan let go of the door handle and made her way across the office to sit in the chair opposite Andrea's.

"What?" her reply was as short as Susan had come to expect. Susan looked up at her and composed herself.

"We found a body, Andrea, a male, a man lying on a bed bunk in business class, in superb condition and Bruce wants you and your team to remove him and bring him here."

Andrea's face lit up, she looked excited; she looked like she had just been given life-changing news and good news at that.

"But there's more, Andrea."

Andrea reclined back in her chair, the good news had a *but,* as it always did.

"After you had examined the first two bodies I had the skulls sent to the Natural History Museum in Washington and I had forensic facial reconstruction done."

Andrea sat forward the look of excitement now replaced by one of confusion and annoyance.

"What? When are they back, Susan, you know I should have been consulted on this, why wasn't I?"

Susan didn't retaliate, partly because she knew Andrea was right, she should have been involved but she was also too tired, she didn't have the energy to fight with her, what little energy and strength she had she would need to return to the hangar and get through the day. She sighed and looked directly into Andrea's eyes. "Yes, you should Andrea and I have them in my tent, they came back a couple of days ago but only Bruce and I have seen them. When we get the body out of the plane we can go get them, bring them over to this site and see if we can't solve this."

Andrea didn't reply, she knew she had scolded Susan enough and given that she and Bruce were running the dig; even she knew she could only push so far.

"Ok, Susan, give me ten, maybe twenty-minutes and I'll get my team ready, then we'll go."

Susan sank into the chair and smiled.

Bruce sat in his tent with the two red boxes placed neatly on his field desk next to his laptop computer. He sat staring at them almost hesitant to connect them and start the download of information he so desperately needed. He wasn't sure what, if anything, they would reveal about why this aircraft was here and part of him wasn't sure if he would even believe it if he heard it.

He plugged the USB lead into the side of his computer and connected the other end to the flight data recorder, the other box was the flight voice recorder that recorded all the communications between the plane and ground control. He always took the information from that one last. There was no real reason for this; he had just always done it that way and he saw no reason why this time should be any different. The laptop chimed as if to congratulate itself for achieving the connection. Bruce moved his hand over the square mouse pad on the laptop until he had placed the cursor over the icon that would launch the download software. His finger hovered over the pad, he looked at the screen of his computer and hit it, instantly the cursor turned into a little egg cup and then the software opened a new window on the desktop. Two pictures appeared, one of a pc and another a basic representation of the red box. A data display line appeared between them and the little arrows that showed that the computer was reading the box started to shuffle between the two pictures. Bruce knew this could take a while depending on how much information there was. He pushed his chair back and stood up. "I'll be back soon," he whispered to the computer and with that he turned and headed for Simon's tent.

Simon had long been up and had had his breakfast when Bruce slapped the flap that formed the door of his tent.

"Simon, you ready?"

"I am, boss. I was waiting for you."

"Ok, I told Susan I would meet her at site bravo; they should have taken our mystery man out of the plane by now."

Simon closed the lid on his laptop and placed it next to him on his bed. Standing up he had an almost guilty look on his face but it was tinged with a bit of sadness as well.

"Everything ok, Simon?"

Simon jerked his head back, he had seen a caring side of Bruce in the past but is was so rare that it still took him by surprise.

"Nothing that can't wait, Bruce, let's go see if they've found anything."

He followed Bruce out of his tent, but just as he left he turned his head and took one last glance at the laptop lying on his bed and with a heavy sigh he turned and left.

Andrea returned to her office where she had left Susan while she assembled her team.

"Ok, Susan, we're good to go."

Susan didn't reply to her verbally, she just acknowledged it with a small nod and stood up. Andrea noticed that she looked worried; she had a distinct look of anxiety on her face like a child who was about to get an injection and knew what was coming.

"You ok, Susan? You look a bit washed out."

"I'm ok, Andrea, I am just dreading going back in there, the atmosphere really isn't nice."

"Don't worry, Susan we will be surgical, we won't spend anymore time in there than we have to."

Susan nodded and followed Andrea out of the office and the tent. Once outside Andrea introduced Susan to the rest of the team, they had commandeered one of the Landcruisers to transport the body back. They climbed in and started the short drive to site charlie. As the truck rolled over the rocky desert floor Susan could see the large blue hangar as they approached it, and she knew what was waiting for them inside, it seemed strange to her now that it didn't bother her that much last night when they had found him, but now she knew he was there, going back seemed somehow wrong and this troubled her deeply.

The Landcruiser stopped outside the entrance to the hangar, small plumes of dust swirled around its fat tyres as they came to a stop. The team climbed out and headed inside, the air-conditioned environment offered a respite from the relentless heat of the sun. The plane now stood clearly in the middle of the hangar, illuminated by the large orange lamps placed around it, the cargo bay was now completely empty and the forensic team that had worked on it were cataloguing what they had removed. Susan started to walk over to Mark Watson who was in charge of clearing the plane.

Susan had worked with Mark on other sites, he was one of the nice guys in his 30s. He lived on his own and as far as Susan knew had no real interests outside of work.

"Mark!" she shouted over to him. Mark looked up and waved at her, he wasn't a big man, standing around 5ft 5", he had a very slim build and short dark brown hair and as usual today he was wearing a pair of blue jeans and a scruffy T-shirt that was clearly too big for him.

"Hi, Susan how are you?"

By now Susan had reached him, she extended her hand and shook his firmly.

"I'm ok, Mark, what have you found so far?"

"Not much, it looks like whoever had lived here used every resource they could, they had cut some of the luggage in half we think to use as water containers, almost everything else is gone."

"Any name tags on the luggage? anything that would give us a clue as who they were?"

"No nothing, Susan, what personal luggage remained was pretty beaten up and worn out, even the extra pieces that didn't belong to the passengers had been used and we think then discarded."

Susan looked disappointed, she really had hoped that she could have gone back to Bruce with some encouraging news, but it seemed this was to be a dead-end as well.

Mark moved closer to her and whispered, "What's the big secret Susan, how come we can't start on the other zones yet?" Susan was desperate to tell him but she knew she couldn't. Whilst Bruce was not her boss she knew she couldn't go against his wishes, even it was out of professional respect. "Sorry Mark, you know I can't tell you that." Mark smiled at her; it was a smile that informed Susan he knew she was hiding something.

"Susan, we're ready to clear the hangar and start in."

Andrea was stood at the rim of the dig ready to descend down towards the bottom of the fuselage.

"Ok, I'm coming."

Susan was glad of the diversion from Mark's questioning. Andrea pulled the bullhorn towards her mouth, "Would all non-cleared personnel now clear the hangar, thank you."

With everyone else, including Mark, out of the hanger it seemed even more eerie than usual. Susan watched as Andrea's team pulled back the huge flap that made up the main entrance and the Landcruiser was reversed in and up to the edge of the dig. Stopping feet away from where they stood its engine died and with that there was no sound, nothing, no-one spoke, and with the flap fastened back in place not even a breeze disturbed them. "Spooky," Andrea said with a hint of sarcasm. Susan turned towards her, "You're not inside yet!" Susan headed down the side of the trench that the plane now stood in and reached the ladder she had climbed the night before. Stretching out her right hand she grabbed it and hauled herself back in to the aircraft. Inside the halogen lights were still lighting up every area of the cargo bay. She guided the team towards the small ladder that would lead them back up to the passenger compartment. Susan pulled the torch off her hip clip and started the short climb. Reaching the hatch, she pushed against it and it jumped out of position. A plume of dust cascaded down over her. She switched the torch on and climbed through the open hatch. One by one the team followed her. Andrea first and then the other four members, the last one passed up the stretcher they had decided would carry the man off the plane and back to Andrea's site.

One by one they turned on their torches and again the galley area lit up in a plume of circular patterns. "Follow me," Susan said, her voice sullen and wobbling as she spoke. The team followed her and soon caught sight of the figure. Susan stepped back and allowed Andrea's team to do their thing. She really didn't want to be part of it and was happy to move back away from them. Andrea reached out a nervous hand. Like

Susan, she had spent years in the field and like Susan, she was used to dealing with fossils and not only partially decomposed corpses. She took a steady grip on the blanket and slowly started to pull it down. The blanket was crisp from years of dirt and dust and cracked and splintered as she pulled it off the body and clouds of dust fell from it. She got it off the side of the bunk and let it drop to the floor. Andrea's light now lit up his face, she couldn't help notice how tranquil the look on his face was, her gaze followed his right arm down his body until she stopped at the hand. It was wrapped in what looked like a handkerchief, she could easily see that is was covered in dry blood, and between the fingers she could see a piece of paper. Carefully she pulled it out and written on it were two words: "Overhead locker."

Andrea turned and held it up to Susan.

"Have you seen this?"

Susan shook her head and started across the middle row of seats towards her.

"No, we didn't disturb anything."

She carefully took the paper from Andrea. Susan knew that even in its unnaturally good condition the paper could be very brittle. She read the words on it and looked at Andrea.

"What do you think?"

"I think we need to look in the locker, Susan."

Susan stepped past Andrea and stood next to the body, its stench reaching the back of her throat, the thick air she struggled with last night now stuck to her; it felt like the air itself had a grip around her and it felt uncomfortable. She reached over the body to the overhead locker and unclipped the catch. Instantly the fragile plastic lock exploded and sent pieces everywhere, the door shifted and a waterfall of dust floated gently down from it, covering the plastic tumbler next to the body along with his left arm and the book it rested on.

Susan put her hand in the locker and started to search round.

Andrea watched as Susan's arm stopped dead. Susan turned to her and bit her bottom lip, her eyes looked focused and slowly she pulled her arm out of the locker and the team watched as she pulled something out. Andrea fixed the beam of her torch on her hand and they could see it was a small brown leather book, sealed in an air-tight plastic wrapper, the type that would be used to wrap up a sandwich and written on the front cover it simply said: "My diary of a life in hell."

Susan looked at Andrea. They shone their torches directly at the book, the intense beams of light cut through the thick dark air and illuminated it.

"Do you know what this could mean, Susan?" Andrea asked Susan with a bleak tone to her voice. But Susan did not answer.

Chapter Five

William and David had reached the edge of the clearing, before they breached the shrub line. They both took one last look at the plane, its bright bodywork contrasting against the dark grey sky and without a word to each other they faced forward again and stepped in to the forest.

The ground beneath their feet felt soft; it was covered in thick moss. The trees were huge; they had looked large from the aircraft but now they were in amongst them they could see just how big they were compared to the trees they had left at home just yesterday, even the foliage seemed out of proportion. The leaves of the ferns were thick and had a massive circumference; the stems were fat and bulky and looked immensely strong. They pushed their way through thick undergrowth until it started to clear a little. The shrubs that had encased them started to thin out and they found themselves on what seemed to be a trail path but there was still no sign of Lynsey or any shred of evidence that she had been brought through this way.

David and William pushed on. Reaching inside his jacket William pulled out his mobile phone and flicked open the cover that doubled as the microphone.

"You don't think that'll work do you?" came a sarcastic comment from David. William just smiled to himself as the signal strength indicator read nothing.

"Worth a try, though," William replied, he closed it and pushed it back into his jacket pocket. The thick undergrowth finally came to an end and in front of them was large slow moving river. "Well, we know where the fresh water is at least," William said as he started to walk closer to it.

"Hold on!" David had a concerned tone to his voice.

"What?"

"Have you never seen a wildlife film? Never seen an unsuspecting animal be taken while it's having a drink?" William stopped and headed back towards David.

"Fair point, what do you suggest?"

David stood looking around for a while, "Let's circle further round, follow it downstream a little round that bend and see what's there."

The two men skirted the thick brush that ran alongside the bank of the river, following its course but keeping themselves camouflaged as best they could with what clothes they had on.

As the bend in the river started to straighten both men stopped in their tracks. On the opposite bank stood a large animal drinking from the river. It was a pale brown colour with large reptilian scales covering its body; its size somewhere between a hippopotamus and an African elephant, but it was neither of these two. On its head it had a large bony crest that had red flashes running up it and two long sharp horns at the top and a third that came out from its beak.

David took hold of William's arm. "You seeing this?"

William nodded, "Do you know what that is?" as William asked the question the huge head lifted from the water and looked directly at the two strange objects that were watching it.

"Shit, what do we do now?" William's voice had a tremble in it.

"Stand still," David's reply was sure and confident and only because of this William did as he was told. The animal snorted and went back to taking huge gulps of water out of the river. Both men physically relaxed, their shoulders slumped and they both breathed a heavy sigh of relief almost in unison. "What did I tell you? he's not bothered about us, William."

Just as William turned and started to form a smile on his face a huge air-shattering roar came from deeper in the trees on the other side of the bank. Immediately the large animal that had ignored them with a dismissive snort lifted its huge head and spun round on its hind quarters, and within a split second it had disappeared into the tree line. The roar came again deafening and terrifying at the same time a cold chill ran down both their backs. William's almost completed smile had turned to a look of sheer panic. "What the fuck was that?" David looked straight in the direction of where the noise came from. He had a look of tremendous concentration on his face.

"David, for fuck's sake." David turned to William, "Quick, come with me." David took hold of William's arm and pulled him back away from the edge of the river and down into the thick brush that surrounded them. Both men lay flat on their stomachs. The roar came again louder, they could feel the air vibrate around them but this time the ground did too.

The trees on the other side of the river shook and swayed back and forth. The crashing sound came again and then again and both men realised with a sense of terror that what they were hearing were footsteps. William turned his head toward David, keeping his profile as low as possible. "What is that, David?" "*Shush!* don't move, don't say a word!" William turned his head back and put his face flat to the ground. His nose pressed against the mud; too terrified to look up, the ground under them shook with each foot step then came another roar. The air in William's ears seemed to split; he pulled his hands up over his ears and dared himself to look ahead. Just as he did it stepped out of the brush line and on to the river bank directly opposite them.

It was massive, standing on two huge thick back legs, the sun that now streamed through the breaking cloud highlighted the huge muscles that supported its colossal frame. David moved his gaze up the animal's body. He saw the tiny arms, no more than small stumps that stuck out of the immense chest but it was when he got to its head he felt a fear grip him, nothing had made him feel like this, nothing in life could have: not even combat situations in the RAF could compare to this. At least then it was almost even and you were in a machine you had some protection but out here they had nothing, all they had was the thick ferns they now hid in and David knew if this thing saw them it would all be over. Its head was colossal, perched on its substantial neck. Its huge teeth jutted out of both its top and bottom lips, massive nostrils smelt the air and snorted as it took huge gulps of water, its small intense eyes scanning in every direction while it drank. With one last mouthful it lifted its head. It stood about 25-30 feet high, water cascaded back down from the opening in its jaws where the huge teeth prevented its lips from forming a watertight seal. It raised its head high and sniffed the air, tilting it from left to right it pulled its neck back and let out another roar. William clenched his hands over his ears again. David watched as it slowly turned and with huge strides it disappeared from where it had come, the vibrations and noise from the footsteps easing as it headed further away from them.

William and David hauled themselves back to their feet. David brushed the dirt from his uniform while William stood staring at the river bank. "That was a Tyrannosaurs Rex, wasn't it?" David stood up straight and nodded to William, "Yes, I've seen enough documentaries and books to know that was a T Rex and I am not hanging around here to see if it comes back."

William breathed in deeply and let it out through puffed-up lips. "I think you're right, I assume you were close to Lynsey, being a work colleague and all, but from what we have seen I think we both know what happened to her.....don't we?"

David nodded but William could tell it was a reluctant one but David knew Lynsey was gone; he had known that when he had first seem the blood and found her shoe but the least he could do was to look for her.

"Ok, William, let's head back, we'll keep to the denser stuff. That way we shouldn't come across anything that big again." The two of them started back towards the general direction of the clearing and the aircraft, they knew once there that not even a T Rex that big would pose much of a danger to them.

"David?" William broke the silence that had accompanied them since they started the return journey.

"What is it?"

"Exactly how much fresh water is on the plane?"

David smiled as he walked along, he had already thought of this inevitable problem but had hoped he could have delayed dealing with it for a least a little while longer.

"The short answer, William, is not much. Water weighs a lot, more than people realise, and it takes a lot of fuel to carry an unlimited amount around on a flight."

"Ok, what's the long answer, David? I think we need to know, because if we are where we both think we are at some point we're going to run out and then we're going to need to come back here."

David stopped and William pulled up alongside him.

"Ok we carry about 30 gallons, less what we've already used for the in-flight drinks and anybody who has washed their hands, et cetera, so honestly your guess as to how much is left is as good as mine."

David set off walking again, pushing his way through the ferns that littered the floor. The sun, ever-brighter after burning off the morning's grey sky, burned its way through the tree canopy covering the floor with dapples of light that changed and moved as the trees did. They came back on to the trail and they knew they weren't far from the clearing. Walking in silence again, both of them were already thinking about reaching the plane and both had stopped concentrating on where they where.

Without any notice or warning the roar came back, they both stopped dead, standing in the middle of the trail, they were both out in the open. William's heart rate increased and it thumped inside his chest. He felt as if his heart would burst from his chest which was getting tighter and tighter, the adrenaline was flowing around his body, saturating his muscles and respiratory system, making him ready for what he had to do.

The roar came again and then the ground shook. Both men turned in circles where they stood, "Where the fuck is that coming from, David?" "Shut up, listen!" David's reply was short and abrupt but it needed to be; this was no time for manners and etiquette.

Again the roar, again the air split in their ears. William pushed his hands hard against his ears again but he couldn't prevent the sound from penetrating deep inside his head. All his primeval senses and fears exploded to life; everything we had long forgotten since living in safe locked homes without the need to hunt and fend for ourselves since we became domesticated, his system became overrun, his legs felt like lead weights, his arms felt heavy and useless, the ground shook again and directly ahead of them, 500-yards or so, the Tyrannosaur burst though the tree line and looked straight at them. David clenched his teeth and whispered to William, "Keep still, don't fucking move an inch!"

William couldn't, he was frozen to the spot. Unlike David, he hadn't dared look at it when they first encountered it at the river but now he had no choice, it was there, it was massive and was looking straight at them. It lowered its head and sniffed the air, its huge tail swung back and forth behind it and its massive legs stayed firmly where they were, its head moved and bobbed from side to side, its small eyes glaring at them, it hadn't seen people before and David could tell it wasn't sure what to make of them, but he also knew that this animal didn't take Lynsey, it was far too big to have sneaked up on her and made in under the plane, and whilst that gave him some relief it also filled him with another thought, if this didn't, what did?

David carefully took a bunch of keys out of his pocket, reaching slowly across, he pushed them in to William's hand and curled his fingers around them. He leaned towards William and whispered, "Get these keys back to the plane, you're going to need them." William didn't get the time he needed to register what David had meant let alone ask him. David placed his right hand on William's left shoulder. Mustering all his strength he pushed William to the side of the trail. William fell to his right crashing through the ferns and foliage falling down the 8-foot drop on that side of the trail. Instantly David turned and ran and with the sudden movements of David's actions the Tyrannosaur set off after him. It bellowed as it started to move its huge bulk forward. William curled up and pulled his head into his chest covering it with his hands, he felt the ground shake and move as it thundered past him. After he was sure it was gone William un-curled himself and started back up the side of the ditch to the trail path. He watched the Tyrannosaur disappear out of view into the dense forest. Pulling himself up he started down the trail back to the plane, running as fast as he could, but it was long time since William had had to run; he had never used a gym and now right at this moment he was regretting it. He could hear the roar from the animal even from this distance. His legs burned and his stomach stitched as he pushed himself gasping for breath, wheezing and coughing he felt as if he was going to pass out, his mouth started to water and his legs slowed to a crawl. Leaning against a tree with his left arm, he doubled over and instantly his body regurgitated all of his stomach's contents, crouching and gasping he wiped his mouth with the back of his right hand. The roar came again, but it was distant. Pushing himself off the tree he started to run again but his muscles had nothing else to give. Now he was staggering, his arms hardly able to hold themselves up by his side, his wrists were limp. He pushed through the scrub into the clearing and he could see the plane just in front of him. *"Sanctuary,"* he thought, he had lost all his dexterity through sheer exhaustion. He banged on the fuselage as best he could as he passed under it and as David had instructed, the cargo door was shut tight. He banged again, "Fucking let me in!" he bellowed with his remaining breath. The door shuddered and slowly it started to open. "Quicker, quicker, come on!" William screamed at them, the door was open enough and the net tumbled down. William snatched at it and started to haul himself inside, he felt arms grabbing him and he was pulled up and into the cargo bay. "Close the door, close the door," William's speech had reduced to no more than a scared whisper. He lay on his back, his body shaking, he turned his head to see the door close and the safety catch pulled across it. With his breath slowly returning to him he pulled himself up onto his elbows. Nick and Amy stood over him. "Where's David?" Amy asked but William couldn't speak, he just looked up at them and shook his head.

David was running as fast as he had ever ran, digging deep, his heart beating and thumping inside him, his lungs strained for every last bit of useable oxygen they could get to power his muscles, adrenaline pumped around him as he burst through the undergrowth. Skipping over tree roots that were sticking out of the ground he didn't dare take a look behind him, he didn't need to, he could feel the ground vibrate and shake every time the Tyrannosaur slammed down one of its huge feet.

David was surprised by the ground it had made up on him even with the 500-yard head start he had and the thick undergrowth that favoured him but it was close.

David could see thick tree line he was heading for; it was within reaching distance. He dug deeper pushing his body to give him every ounce of energy it could; he was almost there, he knew it wouldn't be able to follow inside if he could just get to it, then he felt himself flying through the air. It had happened so quickly he hadn't even felt the contact that had tossed him up like a doll that a child had flung across the room.

Twisting in mid-air his eyes tried desperately to focus on something to make sense of his surroundings as the earth mixed with the sky, but the first thing he could focus on was the ground and it was hurtling towards him fast. His left wrist took the impact and it snapped, the pain shot up his arm and he howled, landing, he tumbled over coming to rest on his back; he opened his eyes to see the huge head of the Tyrannosaur directly over him. It stood at his feet bent over him, its huge tail counterbalancing the weight of it. Slowly it lowered its head down. David reached out with his right hand and searched around feeling for anything he could use, his hand found a rock. Clasping it tightly he rolled his hand over so it was face up in his palm the Tyrannosaur lowered its head down, its nose snorted as it got closer - only inches from his face - as it tried to figure out what this strange thing was it was standing over.

David mustered all the strength he could and swung his right arm over his body bringing the rock crashing down on its left nostril cutting it deeply and instantly releasing a stream of blood. It pulled its head back and let out an almighty growl. David's ears vibrated with the noise, almost stunning him, but he seized his chance; he rolled onto his front and got to his feet. Cradling his left hand he bolted for the treeline now no more than 20-feet away but he wasn't quick enough; it brought his head back down with lightening speed and David was lifted clean off his feet and high into the air. His body held between its huge teeth with his arms pinned by his sides. David turned his head and looked down the left side of its snout, blood ran down out of the wound he had caused. He could see pieces of rotting flesh stuck between its teeth as flies buzzed around it and he knew that shortly that would be all that was going to be left of him. His gaze shifted to its eye, he looked directly in to it and saw an empty soulless eye that knew nothing but violence and brutality. David spat at it and snarled, "Go fuck yourself!" and with that the huge jaws clenched and David's body fell limply into it's mouth.

Nick helped William back on to his feet. "What happened?" asked Nick. William had a morose look on his face, his eyes looked sad and Nick could see he was holding back tears. "It came at us, we thought we'd left it behind, but...it was so big, so fast, I thought David could get clear of it but it was on him in no time."

Nick looked confused.

"What was, what are you talking about?" Nick questioned him further.

"Take it easy," said Amy, she moved next to William and put her arm around his shoulder.

"Can't you see he's upset? whatever has happened has upset him," she scolded Nick.

Nick pulled away and turned to head for the ladder, "Well, all I know is that two of them left and only one has come back!"

William pushed Amy's arm off him, his breath regained. Now he felt angry, angry and frustrated.

"Look!" he shouted to Nick, as he walked away.

Nick stopped and turned round to face William.

"Look, David gave me these keys. I don't know what they're for but he told me to get them back here, then he pushed me down a bank and ran, that was the last I saw of him."

"You said already," Nick replied, "but you haven't said what he ran from."

William shifted on his feet, he looked nervous, he looked like a child that was about to confess to drawing on the wall or some other act that he'd been caught at, "It was a..." he paused.

Nick and Amy drew closer, their gaze held by his pause.

"It was a Tyrannosaur."

Nick jerked his head back and blinked, "A Tyrannosaur?" he questioned William.

"Yes, a T *fucking* Rex, a dinosaur, you know, big and nasty." Then William broke down and started to sob, he fell to his knees. Amy lowered herself back beside him and helped him back to his feet. "It's ok, William, come on, let's get back up top and I'll make you a coffee."

Nick turned and climbed the ladder first. Turning, he helped William up through the hatch and Amy followed behind him.

"William, go and sit there, I'll be over just now." She guided William through to business class and sat him in a seat on the right side opposite where Sarah was sitting with Holly. She turned and saw that William was in obvious distress.

"Holly, I'll be back in a minute."

Holly just smiled and gave a weak wave to Sarah as she stood up and crossed the cabin. As she did Amy came out of the galley, "What's wrong with William?" Sarah asked Amy. "We don't know too much, he said something about David being chased by a dinosaur." "A dinosaur?" Sarah repeated. Amy nodded and placed the hot coffee next to William in the cup holder built into the business class bunks. She sat in the adjacent seat and placed a soft hand on William's forearm.

Amy headed back into the galley where Nick was leaning against the counter. "What did you see, William?" asked Sarah. William sat for a second or two as if he was ignoring her, then slowly he turned his head looking down at her hand and then up to her face; he looked directly in to her eyes and she could see terror in his. "We came..." he started to say through intermittent sobs, "we came across a clearing, it was a river. David stopped me from going too close, he must have been afraid that whatever took Lynsey would still be there." He stopped to take a breath, turning his head straight ahead then bowing it into his chest. "We decided to follow it for a while we walked for about 15-minutes or so and then we saw the first one." Sarah leaned forward so she could see his face, gently rubbing his arm she said, "Saw what, William, what was there?" "An animal, some kind of huge animal. I know it was a dinosaur but I'm not sure what it's called."

"Describe it," another voice came from William's left. A man was stood next to them both. William turned his head and looked up at him. He was a tall man about 6ft 2" or so, black and of a very big build. William thought he must weigh 230lbs or so. He had a bald head and William thought a somewhat mean-looking demeanour - he reminded him of a soldier or even some special forces type. He had noticed him when he boarded the plane but had not taken much notice of him after they had taken off. He knelt down next to William and repeated, "Describe it." William drew his breath again and composed himself, "Well, it was big, on all fours, it didn't stand up like the other one, the...Tyrannosaur," William looked back at the man but he had not reacted to what William had just said, no expression crossed his face. William continued, "it had a large plate sort of thing on its head and three large horns - two on the top of the crest and one on its nose."

The man cut across him, "Triceratops." Sarah turned her attention to him. "A what?" "A Triceratops, it's a herbivore." Sarah rested back in her chair, she had an inquisitive look on her face. "Who are you?" "Marcus Downs, I'm the air marshal on this flight." With that he pulled back his leather jacket that hung over his cream chinos which his navy blue polo shirt was tucked into. Behind the hem of his jacket was his shield clipped onto his belt. "So, how do you know about dinosaurs?" she asked. "Well, if that was what you saw." he turned his attention back to William who interjected, "it was!" Marcus continued, "If that was what you saw, the only animal that I know of that fits that description is a Triceratops."

Sarah turned back to William, putting her hand on his shoulder and giving it a gentle squeeze. "Go on, William, you were telling us what had happened."

He turned back to Sarah and gave her a slight smile. "We watched it for a while drinking from the river, it did see us but didn't seem to be bothered by us being there, but then we heard that roar, that noise, God! it was awful, it sounded like...like..." William struggled to find a fitting description, but he continued, "I've never heard anything like it, the ground shook and then it appeared, it was huge, massive, it went away and we thought we'd left it behind us but it must have circled us because shortly before we got back to the plane it jumped us. David pushed me down the bank and made a run for it. The last I saw of either of them, they were running into the jungle."

William shuffled in his seat and pulled something out of his pocket. Holding out his fist he un-curled it and showed Sarah the set of keys that David had given him. "He gave me these before he pushed me, he said I had to get them back to the plane." "Did he tell you what they were for?" Sarah asked. "Looks like a locker key," Marcus said. "Yeah, but do you see any lockers?" Sarah replied. She snatched the keys from William and took them over to Holly. "Holly, do you know what these are for?" Holly turned her head and looked at the two keys Sarah held out to her. "Looks like the captain's bunk and a locker key." "Thanks, Holly." Sarah returned back to William and Marcus. "She said something about a captain's bunk?" Marcus nodded, "It's behind the flight deck, give me the keys and I'll go check." Marcus took the keys from Sarah and headed forward towards the flight deck and Sarah followed him.

To the left of the flight deck entrance there was a door. Marcus lined the key up and slipped it into the lock that was built into the handle and turned it, with a click the door came ajar and Marcus pulled it towards him. They stepped into the small room that consisted of a bunk bed; the type you often see in documentaries about naval vessels. On the wall that held the door there was a mirror and coat hanger. "No locker," Sarah said. Marcus looked at her and took hold of the mattress. Carefully he lifted it up and under it, built into the bed frame, was a locker. He put the key in and turned it, pulling the locker open. Inside was hand gun. Marcus reached inside and pulled it out, "Jesus," was the only phrase that Sarah could think as Marcus closed the locker and let the mattress fall back onto its frame. Turning, he gestured to Sarah and they left the room. Marcus pulled the door shut behind him but didn't lock it.

They made their way back into business class where William was sitting drinking his coffee and chatting to Amy, who had come back to see how he was. Marcus pulled the gun out of his pocket and showed it to him. "This is what was in the locker."

William put his coffee down and looked uneasily at the gun and then at Marcus.

"Why didn't he take that with him? I mean, if he suspected anything."

Marcus cut across him, "If what you say is real this wouldn't have made any difference. This thing would penetrate a Croc's skin let alone a T Rex!"

"Ok boys," said Sarah, she looked at Marcus, "Look, I know you're a marshal but I think it would be a good idea to keep that out of sight. There is a reason it was locked away, you know."

Marcus smiled. "Relax, I've been around guns since the army but I'll keep tight hold of it and under wraps, ok?"

Sarah smiled, she knew that the "Ok" was a rhetorical one but at least he had listened to her, even if he was a little patronising with his answer.

William stood and took the empty cup through to the galley. Out of nothing more than habit he turned the tap and went to rinse it, but before he turned the tap off, he stood looking at the cup for a few seconds and then placed it in the bin that was built into one of the cupboards.

Sarah had followed him in and had watched with interest what he had just done. "Why throw it away?" "David told me that these planes only carry around 30 gallons of water, given the drinks we've already had and how much has been used washing cups and hands et cetera we don't know how much is left, and when it does run out we have to go back in there, back to the river."

Sarah's expression changed, she had a look of foreboding on her face. William read it and nodded, "Exactly." William left the galley and climbed back into his bunk. By now the sun was setting and he needed the security his bed and blanket seemed to offer him. He lifted the blind a little, just enough to see out of the window from where he was lying. The sun was almost gone, the trees around the plane were now nothing more than forbidding silhouettes that he knew were hiding the monsters of his nightmares and he also knew those nightmares would come again tonight.

The following day William called to the rest of the passengers who were in the economy class cabin and asked them to come through to business class.

Once everybody was gathered around Holly's makeshift bed, William made his announcement.

"Look, I know what David told us the other night about what he had found on the other edge of the clearing and like the rest of you, I was a bit sceptical. But I've seen them, you've all heard by now what happened to David and whether you believe me or not, it did happen! We have to organise ourselves, we have to be ready, we will soon run out of water and food, we're going to need to find fresh supplies at some point and we have to protect ourselves."

William was in full swing, the grand speech he had practised over and over to leave his job was coming in useful now, not exactly what he expected to be saying but he was getting his point across just the same.

"I think we need to disguise ourselves as much as we can."

Nick cut across him, "Disguise ourselves? We're in a huge plane, or had you forgotten that?"

William smiled. "Yes, we are but I don't think the average dinosaur will recognise it as that, do you? What I mean is we should pull all the window blinds down, then if the T Rex comes sniffing around at least it can't see us through the windows."

Marcus interrupted William. "We should also keep an eye open too. I mean, if it can't see us that's fine but we should still be able to see it."

William nodded in agreement, "Ok, we'll take turns sitting in the flight deck and we'll pull the rear blinds up occasionally too, but believe me, even in this plane, if it comes we WILL hear it!"

William looked across at the passengers' faces and everyone of them had the same expression: a mixture of fear, disbelief and scepticism.

He turned to Amy and then moved his gaze to Sarah for reassurance. Sarah smiled at him and nodded as if to encourage him to keep going but William didn't, he couldn't; the sound of the T Rex still haunted him and he'd had enough of trying to be the leader now that David was gone. He turned to Marcus, "They're all yours, Marcus."

Marcus stepped forward and instantly William knew he had done the right thing, the way he moved and stood instantly grabbed the group's attention, then he spoke and it sounded to

William exactly how he imagined a drill SGT to sound.

"Ok, we need to bury Steven before...well, you know."

Nick stepped forward, "If those things are running around out there will it be safe to do so, can't we just dump the body?"

Marcus replied to his question, "If we do that it will draw animals over to us and they'll associate the plane with food. We need to bury him and it needs to be deep and a decent distance from the plane."

Nick accepted the argument and agreed with Marcus. "Ok, if someone will stand guard I'll do it." Marcus looked around at the group of people who now hung on every word he said.

"Look, David and Lynsey are gone, but if we're going to survive here we need to band together to work as a team with one purpose; there can be no individual goals or motives. If we don't stick together we won't make it."

"What can we do while you deal with Steven?" Sarah asked him.

"Ok, we'll bury Steven first thing tomorrow. While we do that make sure the cargo door is locked when we leave and the safety catch is pulled tight. As for tonight, close all the blinds and kill all the lights apart from the ones above where we sleep, that'll save power too. We should also try and stay in the same part of the plane, except Holly, she needs to be comfortable and Sarah, I think you should stay with her."

Sarah nodded, "I will."

"Ok, then that's all I have for now."

With that the group disbanded and headed back through the galley to the economy cabin.

An hour had passed and they had done all that Marcus had asked them to: the cargo door was checked and double-checked, the blinds had been pulled down on all the windows and the remaining passengers were now huddled together in the centre aisle of the economy class seats.

William headed through the darkened cabin passing through the galley and back into business class. He headed over to Sarah who was sitting with Holly. She saw William coming over, He stood beside her and reached out his hand she took hold of it, looking up at him she smiled, "You ok? You've had a funny day."

William sighed, "You're good at understatements!"

Sarah let go of his hand. "So, where are you sleeping tonight?"

"Oh, I think I deserve business class, besides, if Marcus over there can sleep in here, so can I."

They looked over and Marcus was already asleep; laid out on the forwardmost reclining seat.

"Can we trust him with that gun?" Sarah asked quietly.

"Do we have a choice?" William replied.

He turned his attentions to Holly. "How is she doing? She doesn't seem any better."

Sarah took a sad look at her. "She's not, William, she's running a very high temperature and all we have on board are paracetamol."

"Well, you can only work with what you have Sarah, just make her as comfortable as you can I guess."

Sarah smiled and lay back on her bunk. She reached up and switched off the overhead light. William walked over to the other side of the cabin and climbed back into the seat that Amy had put him in earlier. He reclined it down and turned off the light above his head. Reaching across he lifted the blind slightly, outside it was dark, so dark that when he looked backwards he couldn't even see the wings. Another day had slipped by, another day of being a prisoner stuck in this metal container with the memories of yesterday still very fresh in his mind.

Chapter Six

S arah woke to a soft moaning. Her eyes flickered open and just for a split second she thought she was in her own bed and the last three days had just been a weird dream, but as she started to regain consciousness she realised with a heavy heart that she was on board the plane.

She yawned and stretched her arms out from under the blanket that had kept her warm and far too comfortable for her to want to get up. She looked around the cabin; it was still quite dark she could barely make out the interior features, but she could see that Marcus and William were still asleep.

The soft moaning came again, she turned to her left to where Holly was. Sarah could see beads of sweat collecting on her forehead. Sarah reached over and placed her hand on it, she felt warm, too warm. She pulled the blanket down from Holly. The white uniform blouse was wet, she must have been sweating most of the night while they had slept. Sarah pulled her own blanket back and got out of the bunk and headed for the galley. She took out one of the disposable cups which had now become a lot less disposable given the fact they couldn't be easily replaced or replaced at all, and placed it under the cold water tap. Turning it she expected the water to run freely but it didn't; it made a gurgling sound and spat the water out - almost knocking the cup out of Sarah's still half-asleep hand.

She recognised this instantly, she had once lived in an old apartment in New York during a previous job and she knew that there must be air in the system and normally that means there's no water. She took the half-full cup over to Holly. There seemed no point worrying about the water supply right now, she would tell William when he got up though; she knew it would be last thing he would want to hear because it meant a return to the river and after the story he had told them the

111

night before last; that didn't seem a good idea but then neither did running out of fresh water.

When she returned to Holly she was awake; although only just.

"Here, take small sips, Holly."

She took the cup out of Sarah's hand and sipped at the water inside.

"You're burning up, Holly," Sarah said, in the most soothing and calming voice she could muster.

Holly handed her the now empty cup. "I need the toilet, Sarah."

"Ok, honey, I'll help you over."

Slowly, Holly climbed out of her bunk. Sarah could see just how wet Holly was with the sweating she'd done during the night. Her blouse stuck to her as did her dark blue skirt and as she walked to the toilets, Sarah could hear her tights rubbing.

"I think we should get you changed, Holly. You go to the toilet and I'll head down to the cargo bay and try and find you something that'll be more comfortable."

"Ok," replied Holly.

Sarah helped her into the toilet and then headed back to the hatch in the galley. Slowly she pulled it open and climbed down the ladder, she felt for the lights and found them. With a click the fluorescent tubes flickered and then bathed the hold in a harsh bright light. Sarah headed over to the left-hand side where she remembered David telling them that was where the passengers' luggage was kept. She found her own bags and pulled them down from the rack. She unclipped the latches and flipped the lid open. She sat in front of the case and looked at the present that was laid on top of her clothes. She smiled to herself and brushed her hands over it. The present was for her niece who was turning thirteen. She had taken ages deciding what she would like when she became a teenager and now after all the thinking and pondering it seemed that her niece would never receive it anyway. Sarah pushed the present to one side and dug through her clothes until she found the PJs she had brought for the short stay she had planned at her sisters. She closed the lid and returned the case to its resting place on the rack; she turned and headed back up to the galley.

William was starting to stir as the first light of the day started to find its way through the small cracks where the blinds didn't quite fit snug against the window frames.

He turned in his bunk and opened his eyes. Looking into the cabin he could see that Sarah and Holly were gone from their bunks. Stretching, he got out and made his way to the galley.

As he stepped through the curtain he saw Sarah coming up from the cargo bay holding her clothing. "Morning, Sarah, how are you?"

"Not bad, William, I had to go and get some clean clothes for Holly, she's burning up and her clothes are soaking from sweating."

"Do you think she'll come out of it?" William asked.

Sarah shrugged her shoulders, "To be honest, I don't know. I had a look at the wound when you and David had gone looking for Lynsey and..." She stopped.

"And what, Sarah?" William prompted her to continue.

"Well, it looks to me as though it's badly infected, and we don't have any antibiotics."

William nodded in acknowledgement, "Ok, Sarah, keep an eye on her."

As Sarah replaced the hatch, William turned the tap to get a drink of water but nothing happened.

"I was going to tell you about that, William, once you were up."

"What do you mean?" he replied.

"I got a drink this morning for Holly and only managed to get half a cup, I think we're out."

William tossed the cup into the sink and rested both hands on its side, his head sunk in his shoulders. "Shit, you know what that means, Sarah, don't you?"

Sarah sighed, "I think I do but I know it's not where you want to return to."

William took a sideways glance at her. "As I said, a master of understatement!"

Sarah smiled and left the galley to head back to Holly, who she had left in the toilet.

Sarah knocked on the door of the locked toilet. "Holly, you there?"

"Yeah," came a short and weak reply.

"Unlock the door, honey, I've brought you a change of clothes."

With a click the door unlocked and Sarah passed in her PJs. Holly took them and the door shut tight again.

William made his way into the economy cabin. The other passengers had started to wake up. Amy and Nick were already up and looking out of the windows on each side of the cabin. William headed over to Nick first and sat next to him.

"Anything?"

Nick turned to confirm whose voice he had just heard.

"Nothing, William, it's all quiet, the weather looks good but I can't see anything moving."

He turned and reached past William.

"Amy, you see anything out there?"

"Nothing, Nick, nothing at all."

Marcus appeared through the curtain and made his way to where Nick and William sat. He sat in the middle row adjacent to them.

"So what's the plan today?"

William answered his question. "Where do I start? we need to bury Steven today without delay or he could infect the plane and there's another problem." William leaned towards Marcus so that he could whisper, "it looks like we've run out of water, which means we're going to have to go and get some!"

William relaxed back but he could tell by the look on both their faces that they didn't like the idea any more than he did.

Nick turned from his viewing spot. "Could we not search elsewhere for a water supply?"

William thought about it for a few seconds but as much as he wished they could he knew it wouldn't help them.

"The problem is that I reckon wherever we go around here there's a good chance there'll be something out there that wants to eat us, and I thought of something else last night."

"What's that?" asked Marcus.

"It seems to me that there is no way that T Rex could have sneaked up on Lynsey and taken her out of the cargo bay as David thought. She would have heard it, everyone on the plane would have heard it, but also there is no way in hell that it could have fitted under the plane."

Marcus shook his head. "That's good news isn't it?"

William gave him a disdainful look. "Think about it, Marcus, if the T Rex didn't get her, then what the hell did?"

William could tell by the look on Marcus's face that the penny had dropped.

"Shit," said Nick, "and I've had another thought."

"What?" asked Marcus directly.

"Whatever took her may now think of the plane as a place to eat."

"Agreed," said William.

Marcus sat quietly for a few seconds and joined in. "Look, I think we need to get organised, we may be smaller and we may be easy prey out in the open but there's a reason mankind ended up at the top of the food chain."

"And what's that?" asked Nick.

"Our brains. In nature we're quite weak you know, we don't really stack up against anything in terms of strength and speed, but we're much cleverer and in the end that's what counts."

"Yeah, if we had the technology with us maybe a couple of SUVs, hunting rifles, maybe a tank, but we've got nothing except that small hand gun you have and you already said that won't do much to a big animal."

Marcus shook his head like a teacher who was getting frustrated with a student who just couldn't get to the answer.

"You're not hearing me. We have a ready-made castle here, a safe house. I don't think anything here is big enough to be much of a threat to the plane, agreed?"

Both Nick and William agreed.

"Ok then, what we need is to work out how we can minimise the risk while we are out of the plane looking for food and water."

"Ok, Rambo," joked William, "how the hell do we do that?"

Marcus smiled. "I prefer Hannibal from the A-Team."

William managed a small laugh. "Ok, Hannibal, you're going to build a tank from the cases in the cargo hold and I suppose Face here will chat the T Rex up." He pointed to Nick, who laughed with him.

Amy came across from her seat, "What's going on here? You seem to be having a laugh."

"We've decided we're the A-Team, Amy, who'd you like to be?"

"You're mad, the three of you," she smiled.

William sat back in the chair. "This is the first time I've smiled since I left my flat."

Sarah got Holly back to her bunk. She had changed her blankets and pillows and given her some more paracetamol for the constant pain she felt in her arm. Holly had almost gone straight back to sleep and Sarah knew from her time helping out in the local hospitals and health centres that this was not a good sign but she also knew there was nothing else she could do for her. Either her body would fight it or this place would claim another life. Once she knew that Holly was asleep, Sarah got up and went looking for William.

Pushing her way through the curtains she found him towards the back of the economy class still sitting with Marcus, Nick and Amy.

"Hi, everyone," Sarah said as she approached the group.

"Hi, Sarah, how are you this morning?" asked Marcus.

"I slept ok but I'm worried about Holly, she's not getting any better."

None of them seemed to react to this news which took Sarah back a little but it seemed by the conversation they carried on with that they were discussing plans around going hunting, and upon reflection, Sarah thought that was as important.

"Anything I can do to help?" Sarah asked them.

William turned to her, "I think if you stay here and see to Holly and just reassure the rest of the group."

Sarah cocked her head as if she was confused about something. "That sounds to me like you're going back out there, William?" William sighed again. "I am, Sarah, I know the way, besides, this time we'll be ready and there will be four of us, plus Marcus has his gun."

Sarah just nodded her head. Really, she knew that she had no reason or right to ask him or even expect him to not go and with that she stood up and made her way back to Holly's seat.

Marcus looked at William. "Anything going on between you two?"

"No! what gives you that idea?"

"Just the way she reacted when you told her you were going back to the river."

"Ok then," Nick interrupted much to William's relief, "I guess we should get organised."

William agreed, the sooner he could leave Marcus's line of questioning about Sarah behind him the better.

"We should head to the cargo bay and see what we can use." The group agreed with William and they set off to the cargo bay, the fluorescent lights still illuminating it in a harsh white light.

The four of them headed over to the right side of the bay and unclasped the tie straps that held the bulky luggage and other storage containers in place. One by one they emptied and went through the boxes and luggage to see what, if anything, could be used from the excess cargo the plane was carrying.

As Marcus had suspected, there wasn't much that would be of any use as far as they could see. Nick picked up a large bag containing a full set of golf clubs. "Anybody for a game?" he chuckled. "They could be a good weapon if used correctly," Marcus stated.

"Well, if you're so good with them I'll swap you them for the gun," replied Nick.

"Now, now, boys!" Amy interrupted them, "lets just find things we can all play with."

William smiled to himself. He moved a box to one side and found two shovels. He sat back, the find had brought back to him the grizzly task they had yet to complete. "Guys, I've found some shovels," he announced to the group. Nick understood the statement and placed the golf clubs back against the side of the fuselage. "I guess we should just get on with it." he said.

"Nick, you're right, that would be the right thing to do; all things being equal but they're not, and I, for one, am not going out there without something to protect myself," Marcus replied.

"It's alright for you, Marcus, you have a 9mm stuck in your trousers," Nick said.

"Yes I have but as I have said, Nick, it won't penetrate a thick hide and it only has one clip which means around 20 rounds and I don't know about you but I want better odds than that!"

Amy broke their attention to each other again, "Look this is not an army or air force plane - it's a civilian one and we should be grateful that Marcus has at least got something that might scare whatever is out there away and that might buy us enough time to get away.

William jumped up. "That's it, we can scare them, these planes carry rafts, right?"

"Yes," Marcus replied.

"And rafts have flares, yes?"

Marcus smiled and nodded, "Good thinking, let's locate the rafts and take the flares."

The group found the rafts and each took the flares from them giving them two each.

"Ok, only use these when you're up close and personal - not from 200-feet or it might not have any effect," Marcus told them.

Now feeling somewhat protected the group took the shovels and Steven's body and placed them next to the door. Nick started to crank the handle. As he did the door slowly opened and William could feel himself becoming more and more uneasy. He had dreaded this moment coming even though he knew it would. There was no way he could have stayed in the safety of the aircraft from now until, well, whenever until was. At some point he would have to go back out and it might as well be now. Nick opened the door as far as necessary. Marcus pushed the shovels out of the open doorway, followed by the body. Amy scowled at him, "Bit of respect, Marcus."

"Ok, Amy, you carry it out over your shoulder while you climb down the net!"

She just looked away. She had hated the contempt with which he had treated the body, but she knew under these circumstances it was the only way to do it.

Nick pushed the net over the side and looked at William. "You ok?" William didn't really react; he just lowered himself over the side and started down the net. When the three men were on the ground Nick gave Amy a thumbs up and she winched the door closed again.

The men stood and looked around them; still standing under the aircraft.

"Ok, let's get this over with, we'll bury him over there." Marcus pointed to a random spot around 250-feet away from the plane and they started out.

Marcus and Nick carried the body and William followed behind with the shovels and following Marcus's instruction; each of them surveyed a different angle as they walked.

"Ok, this will do," Marcus announced. "I'll stand guard, you two dig. You need to be about at least 6-feet down," said Marcus.

William agreed. Out of the three of them, Marcus had military training; which he assumed included standing guard and *anybody can dig a hole*, he thought. It wasn't long before they had dug down, the ground wasn't that hard. The thick mossy grass that covered the surface was easy enough to break through and the sharp edges of the shovels soon broke up the ground underneath.

William and Nick laid the shovels down and took each an end of the wrapped body. They took three swings with it and it dropped it into the hole, lying it almost perfectly flat.

"Do we need to say something?" William asked.

"You're a religious man, William?" asked Nick in return.

"No, Nick, not really, but it just seems that we should."

William had a sad tone in his voice. "It's not as if I had the chance to say anything to him."

"Ok," said Nick, "a quick word, this place creeps me out." The three of them stood around the grave looking down on the body wrapped in blue polythene sheets tied up with string.

They each said whatever they could remember from the various funerals they had attended for relatives and friends over the years and then stood for a minute's silence. As they did the sounds from this strange place became ever more apparent. The air was warm and thick. William had been outside twice now and it still felt strange, almost taking his breath. It reminded him of waiting for a tube train, standing on the small platform deep underground where the air was warm and still until the train arrived, when it pushed the air along in front of it and in turn the air pushed against you. The sounds that surrounded them from all sides were strange eerie sounds that haunted them, even in this bright daylight: cries, songs, howls and the infrequent menacing growls.

William felt as if he was being watched from all sides. None of them said anything as they piled the earth over the body. Once they had finished only the disturbed earth marked the grave. "Poor bastard," remarked Marcus, as they turned and headed for the plane.

Chapter Seven

Bruce and Simon had made their way to Andrea's office. As they pushed their way into the tent, the body that had met them last night was now laid on the examination table where the first three bodies had been placed after they had been discovered in site bravo.

Both men stopped and looked down on the body almost in unison. Now, out here in the bright light of the large illuminated tent, every detail of this unfortunate soul was on show.

Bruce folded his arms across his chest and stood motionless. Simon stood beside him, placing his hands on his hips. He wasn't very comfortable like this but the only other thing he could think of doing with his hands right now was putting them in his pockets; which somehow seemed disrespectful to him, or copy Bruce, but that just felt wrong.

Bruce turned his head and glanced sideways at Simon. "Ever seen a dead body like this before?"

Simon shook his head. They had seen too many dead bodies during their time in this job, poor, ill-fated souls that had boarded the plane with no idea what was about to happen or that it would be their last day on earth, but they had never seen one like this before, not under these circumstances, not like this.

"Bruce!" He heard the voice and turned to see Susan standing in the doorway of Andrea's makeshift office. "Over here, Bruce and bring Simon, you BOTH need to see this!"

Bruce tapped Simon on his shoulder and nodded his head in the direction of Susan. "C'mon, Simon, let's see what the fuss is over."

Bruce had a flippant tone, mainly because he was sure that there could be no more surprises from this plane, there could be nothing else for it to throw at them, but he was wrong and it was only a short walk before he realised it. Bruce pushed the office door open and Simon followed him through it.

"Hi, ladies," Bruce said. Andrea looked up at them from behind her desk and turned her gaze to Susan. Bruce could tell - even through Andrea's usual hard looks - that she was spooked, something wasn't right.

"Shut the door, Simon," said Susan.

"What's up?" asked Simon.

The two women looked at each other then Susan pulled the clear plastic wallet that contained the book from her pocket. She laid it on the desk in front of them both. "We found this, this morning as we were taking him out."

Bruce leaned forward to get a clearer view. He read the words written on the front and instantly sat back in his chair. Simon's eyebrows lowered. "What's up? What is it?" Susan turned the book to an angle that Simon could see better. "Shit!" Was the only exclamation that Simon could think of. Bruce looked at Susan. "You read it?" She shook her head. "No, not yet, Bruce. We waited for you two to get here."

Bruce reached out to the book, placing his right hand on the edge of it, he pushed it slowly over to her side of the desk.

Susan reached out in return and picked the packet up. She carefully pulled the plastic seal open. A hiss filled the silent office as the ancient air escaped its incarceration. She put her hand in the bag and pulled out the little brown book . She folded the book open at the first page and they watched as her eyes scanned the page for a few seconds. Her gaze lifted from the book and back to the three of them then back to the book.

If you're reading this then you've found me. I don't know how long it has been since we crashed here. I don't even know where here is or when this is! Sounds stupid, I know, but if you had seen what I've seen, heard and had to do what I've had to do, it would make sense.

I've tried to log this as best I can. I've never kept a diary, never seen the point really, my life has never been interesting enough, but I hope at least to explain why we're here and that it brings peace to someone sometime, more peace then we have found here.

After the event, that's what the pilot, David, called it, we crashed landed. We knew it was the wrong place but none of us said anything - at least not for the first night. I think we were all too tired or relieved that we had survived whatever had hit the aircraft. At least most of us had survived. It was the next day when everything started; that was when we all knew we were in trouble and deep down we all knew we would never leave this place, never get back home and never see our families again; at least those with families. I don't know how long we've been here; there are only four of us left now. I know deep down the lucky ones died quickly!

David came through to the cabin; he called us all together, told us that we couldn't take off again and that we would have to wait for help to come but it didn't; it never came and we knew it wouldn't! He told us that his co-pilot, Steven, had been killed when the plane hit and one of the cabin crew, Holly, had smashed her arm during the event.

Bruce interrupted Susan, "Holly? Susan, that's our Jane Doe and I'm guessing Steven must be John!" Susan nodded and returned her gaze to the book...

He told us when he had gone outside to look at the damage to the plane, Lynsey had been taken by something, I still don't know what but something made a mess of her.

We buried Steven and went looking for Lynsey with David but he didn't make it back, something got him, too!

The nights are the worst here. You can hear them walking around outside. The noises they make are awful, worse than you can imagine, whoever you are!

You can hear them sniffing around the plane. The big ones sniff at the windows but they have never figured out that they could be broken. Sometimes they scratch at the metal under the plane; prodding it, poking it, trying to get at us inside. Sleep has become a luxury: like toilet paper, soap or even food.

The days aren't much better; the air is thick and hot, so damn hot and the smell! God, it's putrid especially when we go into the forest. We know we're being watched all the time something is stalking us; waiting for its chance to strike, to take one of us. There are times I wish for death, for it to come quick from behind so that I don't feel it or see it, but it never does.

Susan stopped reading and looked up at the group, "Jesus Christ!" "What the hell were they going through?" Bruce pointed his index finger towards the book, "Carry on, Susan!"

We went hunting today. Caught the usual small lizard thing we seem to eat most days; don't know what it's called, no-one here does, could have done with some kind of monster expert with us really.

We killed a big one the first time we went hunting but not since. Sometimes we're lucky we come across a big one that's died or been killed by an even bigger one. When we do we cut as much off as we can and run before whatever did kill it comes back! We only had one vegetarian with us but that didn't stop him becoming a meal either, I assume anyway. He left with the rest of them. We'll never see them again.

I've sat and thought, I shouldn't be here, I should be at home or at work, stuck in the traffic or watching crap on the TV. These creatures have no right to hunt us; we are at the top of the food chain...at least we were!

Susan slowly closed the book and placed it on her knee. Bruce could see her eyes watering. "Monsters?" Bruce asked. "Surely he must have recognised them as dinosaurs, I know I would have!"

Andrea replied with her usual candour, "I think if they were chasing me and making my life a living hell I would be tempted to call them monsters as well!"

Bruce smiled and nodded, "Guess you make a good point."

"You going to read more, Susan?" Simon asked.

"In a little while, Simon," she replied. "To be honest, I need a break from it."

"Me too, and I need a coffee as well, why don't we meet in my tent around eight tonight? the site will be quieter then," Bruce added.

Bruce and Simon stood up and left the office. Susan watched them go.

"Andrea! Did you notice how Simon was acting?"

"He seemed a bit preoccupied to me," Andrea answered her.

"Me too, you think it's anything we should be worried about?"

"No, I think we're all a little bemused by this whole situation and out of the four of us he is the least experienced."

Susan looked at her in a quizzical way. "Experienced? I don't think any of our experience has a bearing on this one, do you?"

Susan stood up, holding on tight to the little brown book, "I'll see you at eight."

William, Marcus and Nick reached the cargo bay door and knocked three times. It shuddered and started to open, at least far enough for the net to come down and the three of them to climb inside. Once in, William noticed a wide-eyed look about Amy. She was standing towards the back of the cargo bay. "Come see what I found, boys." They looked at each other and headed towards her. She pointed down at a large box.

Lifting her left foot she flipped off the lid, "Tada!" she sang. William bent over the box. Pulling the cover off it he could see what her excitement was about. Inside the large box was a supply of camping equipment. "Jackpot!" William said. He started to pass out the contents to Nick and Marcus. They laid it all out on the cargo deck floor, checking to see what they had.

"Ok then, we have: a tent, two torches, two lanterns, a camping stove, water flasks, blankets, a ground sheet and a pan set. Not too bad, lads!" Marcus said excitedly.

William calmed the excitement down. "I think we should keep this between us for now."

"Keep what between you?" A loud voice came from behind them. The four of them spun round to see a group of the remaining passengers standing in the cargo bay just in front of the galley ladders. Marcus Nick and William formed a line in front of Amy and the large spread of camping gear while she stuffed it hurriedly back in to the container.

"Not much, really," Marcus replied, "why, what's it to you?" he asked them.

Amy noticed Marcus. He was tightening his hand around the grip of his gun that was stuck in the back of his trousers. The spokesman for the group stepped a little further forward.

"Because, since we landed here - wherever this is - we haven't been told Jack shit!" He pointed to William, "You went off with the captain and he didn't come back, the other stewardess has gone missing and now the water's off, so we want answers and you four have been sneaking around here like you own the goddamn plane!" His face became redder and redder as he spoke.

Marcus pulled the gun an inch further out of his pants. As he did, Amy stepped from behind them; placing her hand on Marcus's, stopping the gun from coming out further.

"Look, Mr..."

"John," he interrupted her.

"Look, John," she continued, "we don't know much more than you. We've had a look around here, buried Steven and that's about it."

"Yeah! and what about him?" he pointed at William again.

"Where's the captain? We need to get out of here and get home. I have to get home; my wife will be worried sick."

William stepped forward. "David was chased by an animal, he died to save me. He pushed me over and ran and it ran after him."

John clenched his jaw, "What ran after him? a lion, a fucking bear, what?"

William looked down at the floor and then directly into John's eyes. "You heard what I said when it happened. A T Rex, a dinosaur; a fucking big lizard. What do you want me to tell you?"

John laughed but William knew it was a sarcastic laugh.

"A T Rex? What? you think we're all stupid do you? You think only you four can make decisions about things? well you aren't doing it for me and the rest of us agree!"

As he spoke the other group members nodded and groaned in agreement.

"Oh, is this right? Tell me, John, what do you do for a living then?" Marcus asked.

"I'm a marketing manager, and I know how to get things done, and right now we've decided that walking out of here is the best thing to do!"

William stepped forward in front of Amy. "Walk out? did you not hear me explain about David? Is none of what you have been told making any sense to you?"

"Load of bullshit and we ain't listening anymore, we're going, but first we're taking what we want. You four can stay here with that busted stewardess upstairs and her nurse!"

Marcus pulled the gun, pointing directly at John's head. "You go, you take fuck all!"

John stepped back, a look of shock then fear swept across his face.

Amy moved closer to Marcus, placed her left hand on the gun barrel and pushed it down so that it faced the floor. "Look, John, you want to leave you can and anybody else that wants to. You've been told about David, if you don't believe it that's up to you, but if you go you're not leaving us with nothing. We'll divide it and then you can go."

John relaxed his face and his stance. He nodded at Amy's compromise.

Marcus gave Amy a sideways glance and put the gun back into the back of his trousers. John turned to the group behind him as if to bask in some sort of victory over them. As he did Marcus whispered in Amy's ear, "Happy?"

She turned her back on the group so that she could talk to Marcus without being heard or seen. "Look, we're going to need that gun of yours for something worse than that fat bastard and some cronies. Let them go, you know they won't survive out there anyway." Marcus took a deep breath and walked back to the large container that held the camping gear.

"Ok then, it's decided," John shouted back over to them.

"We're going to collect the stuff out of our overheads then we'll come back down and split this stuff."

William shouted at him with a concern in his voice, "Now? The day is half-way through; you won't get very far before it gets dark. You've heard the noises at night, things moving outside. Why not wait till morning?"

Marcus didn't give John time to answer. "Let them go. Tonight, tomorrow night, they'll be outside at some point so why worry."

"Exactly," John answered. "We'll go today then that way we can send the emergency crews back for you sooner." John smiled at William as he said it and continued, "that is unless your dinosaur finds us, eh, William?"

"Yeah, that's right, and when it does just remember I tried to warn you before it eats your fat arse." With that William turned his back on him and walked towards Marcus; who was stood over the camping equipment as if he was on guard duty.

Marcus smiled at him. "Marketing executives? Typical arsehole." William smiled and nodded at him.

As John and the group headed up the ladder back to the cabin Marcus started to unload the container. "Here!" he said, "put these lanterns away and leave them just the one torch, they can take the tent and the groundsheet, a blanket and two water flasks."

"They'll need more than that," Amy protested.

"Yes they will, Amy, assuming that they will survive out there, but you and I know they won't so we're not giving them equipment that we can't afford to lose for it to be left abandoned when they're all dead!"

Amy didn't like it but she knew he was right and she knew there was no way they could go looking for it. William and Nick looked at each other. There was a mutual agreement between them that they were glad Marcus was staying with them.

The ladder rattled again as John and the rest of the group climbed down it. Amy stepped back behind Marcus, who now stood in the middle of Nick and William with the equipment they had placed for them, in front of them by the door.

"Is this it?" John asked.

"That's all we can spare. It's not that cold at night, I'm sure you can build a fire, you've got the tent!"

John stared at Marcus for a few seconds and then his eyes admitted defeat. Even with the majority of the passengers behind him, John knew Marcus had the gun and that weighted it in his favour.

"Can we take our own baggage?" A voice from behind John asked. William answered her, "You can take your own stuff but I'm not sure you will want to carry it all. I would just take what you need."

With that, one by one, the group moved over to the luggage racks and started to pull down their bags. Amy stood and watched as the bags were ransacked. She felt a wave of sadness wash over her. "This isn't the way we should be behaving, we should be sticking together, helping each other." Her whisper found William's ear and he turned his head towards her. He could see that her eyes had started to water and with that William's started, he couldn't hold himself back any more. He stepped forward and grabbed John's arm. "Listen, you can't go out there, you won't last, you won't make it!" He had a sense of desperation in his voice. John pulled his arm away.

"Don't try and scare us, you want to stay here and rot? so be it, but we're going to find help and get back to our families."

William's voice started to break up. Amy could hear the anxiety coming through in it. "Listen all of you, there are things out there, they took Lynsey and David. I saw them. Please don't go."

This time John didn't answer William, he just turned his back on him and hurried his group. "C'mon everybody let's just go with what we have, it won't be that far."

William went to move forward again but Marcus grabbed his wrist and pulled him back. "Leave it, William, they won't listen," he whispered to him.

The group headed for the cargo bay door with John at the front. Raising his index finger and pointing at the door he looked at Marcus with a look of contempt on his face. "Can we go now?..PLEASE!" he said to Marcus and smiled.

Marcus didn't even return the look to John. He simply moved to the crank handle and started to open the door. Once it was half open he tossed the net out and turned to John. As he did he waved his hand towards the door as if he was an usher at a wedding and he was directing John to the bride or groom's side. "Be my guest!" he said.

John got down onto his hands and knees and turned to lower his legs over the side of the plane. Grabbing hold of the net he shuffled the rest of his oversized body over the side and started the climb down.

One by one the remaining passengers followed him and all William could do now was stand and watch them go, his arms crossed, as a single tear ran down his cheek. Amy put her arm around him and gave it a squeeze. "There was no more you could do, William, it was their choice."

"Yeah, but they're still going to die, Amy. I'm off to see how Holly is." He pulled out of Amy's hug and pushed through the group that were still waiting to climb down the net to what William, Nick, Marcus and Amy knew would be certain and probably a terrifying death

William came out of the galley and headed over to where Holly was lying with Sarah. "How is she?"

"She's still running a temperature and the cut on her arm has become infected." As she spoke, Sarah pulled the blanket from Holly's arm and peeled back her dressing. Holly didn't react a lot; she winced and groaned softly but that was all and William knew that this wasn't a good sign.

"Here, take a look," Sarah said.

William looked down at the wound. The first thing that hit him wasn't the discolouration of it or the skin that was drying and cracking around the open wound; what he noticed first was the smell. It was the smell of dead and rotting flesh and whilst William, like most people, hadn't experienced this before the last few days, he now knew exactly what it smelt like.

Steven had had the same smell about him when they buried him earlier and now Holly had it.

William sat back on the floor next to Sarah's seat and rested his head against the side of her chair. He pulled out his phone and looked at the display. "It's only 3:30 pm and already the day has been shit, I wonder what else could go wrong!"

"William!" Amy's voiced shattered the uneasy silence. "William, Marcus wants you down here."
William looked up at Sarah and smiled. "I had to ask."
It was a tired and weary look that he had on his face. It reminded Sarah of the look a defeated person gave you when almost everything that could go wrong had, and all they wanted to do was curl up and ignore the world.
Hauling himself up, he headed back towards the galley where he could see Amy's head poking out of the open hatch.
"What is it, now?" he asked her.
"They're leaving," she answered and then she disappeared back into the hold.
William climbed down and headed towards the half open cargo door. He squatted down next to it so that he could see the group as they stood on the ground outside the aircraft ready to leave. "Don't go, please think of what I've said," William pleaded with them one more time.
As he did, John turned to look up straight into William's eyes. "Goodbye." And with that the group of sixteen set off, soon disappearing from the view William had out of the door.
He jumped up and raced back up the ladder heading over the left side of the aircraft. He pulled up a window blind and through the now dirty water-stained window, watched as they moved across the open ground and vanished into the jungle that surrounded them. As he did, he could hear the now unmistakable clank of the cargo bay door closing. He sank back in the seat, sighing to himself. He knew he would never see any of them again. Amy sat next to him. "You really couldn't have made them stay, you know." William didn't turn

to her. He continued to look out of the window; even though the group had long gone. "I know, Amy, but that doesn't change anything, they're still all going to die. I suppose we can thank God there was no children on this flight."

Amy didn't really answer him she just smiled even though William couldn't see it and rested her head on his shoulder.

Marcus and Nick made their way back into the galley, pulling the hatch cover shut as they did. Marcus looked at the wall-mounted clock above the microwave oven, "4:12pm." He leaned against the galley worktop. "It's too late to go get water now; I doubt we'll be back in time. We'll head off first thing."

John was at the front of the group slowly pushing his way through the thick shrubs and foliage that they had stumbled in since leaving the open plane. Next to him walked Victoria Downs. Vicky, as she liked to be called, was a legal secretary heading home following her mother's illness. She a was a tall, thin woman with sharp facial features, long dark hair and a flare for designer clothes and make-up. "Why won't this stupid thing work?" she moaned. John turned his head to see what she was making such a fuss about as she walked. Vicky slapped her cell phone with one hand while pressing down on its touch screen with the other.

"You don't really expect that to work, do you?" John said with a sarcastic tone.

"The man in the shop told me this would work anywhere I go," she snapped back.

"Yeah, but I doubt he thought you were going here!"

John looked at her while he spoke to her. He had a big grin on his face but it wasn't an affectionate one, it was one of victory, the type of annoying glance he would give after pulling some useless fact out of the air to make a point or prove someone wrong.

Vicky pushed the phone back into her small shoulder bag

and dropped back away from John.

After a further time pushing through the ever-thickening shrubs and plants they entered a clearing. It was a track that ran as far as they could see in either direction. The group stopped in a line along its edge with John in the middle of them. He noticed they were all looking at him, all looking to him for guidance and instructions. Suddenly he felt important as he did back in the office when he sat behind the over-sized meeting desk with his focus group trying to think of new ways to say the same things again and again for each new product; that none of us knew we needed, and if truth be told, we don't. But it didn't matter where he was, he considered himself a born leader, a cool-headed individual who could lead, given any situation, and after completing the previous weekend's outward bound team-leading course; now he was an expert in field survival as well, or so he thought! Standing as tall as his 5ft 6" frame could manage, he announced to his assembled followers that they would camp here.

After a couple of hours they had managed to erect the tent and build a couple of camp fires with the matches Vicky had had in her bag to support her smoking habit. John was sat by one of the fires when one of the group approached. "Hey, John, can I ask you something?" came a nervous sounding request. John smiled. He liked to keep his team on their toes, he liked to be unpredictable so that they would always be nervous around him; at least it worked for him in the marketing world so why not out here? He looked up and saw a man standing just off to his left. "What is it?" John answered him with a cool tone. "What exactly are we going to do for food and water?"

John turned back towards the fire, holding his hands up in front of it, warming his palms.

"Well, ermm, sorry, what's your name?"

"Oh, it's Tony," came the reply.

"Well, Tony, tonight we won't do anything, its not safe to go wandering, there could be ditches or water you can't see or even one of William's dinos; so just sight tight and we'll have breakfast in the morning."

John didn't look at Tony when he gave him the answer, he couldn't be bothered and Tony didn't reply, he just turned and headed back towards his wife, who he had left sitting around one of the other small fires.

The group had a restless night. Used to the comfort the plane had given them since their forced landing here, the ground proved to be hard and uncompromising, and the sounds of the night that William had told them about; they had all heard while they were in the plane but in there, they didn't matter; out here in the open with no protection they seemed to take on a new menace, and Tony was convinced something was out there in the absolute dark of this place and it was circling them, checking them out and waiting for its chance.

Daylight broke on the group and they had all made it through their first night outside of the protection of the plane. John had claimed the tent for himself whilst the rest had huddled around the fires to keep warm and offer some deterrent to unwanted guests through the cold dark cloudless night.

In the morning they packed up and headed south down the trail. It wasn't long before they arrived by the bank of a large river. John turned in the general direction of Tony, the man who had annoyed him the previous night. There were a few reasons why he had annoyed him but the main reason was that John had been so preoccupied with getting as many people off the plane to follow him, finding water had slipped his mind and Tony had left him feeling embarrassed and stupid. "I give you water," he announced. "Now fill the canteens and water bottles we brought with us and then we'll keep moving." One by one the group made their way to the edge and started to crouch as they filled their containers.

From under the water the predator could see the line of individuals clearly; slowly it moved forward camouflaged by the water reflecting the sun which now shone high in the sky directly behind them causing a blinding sheen across the surface. It made its way down the line until it reached the end figure. Evolution had taught it to always take the end one, it was the least protected and usually the weakest.

The group was spread out thinly along the river bank. They were all concentrating on getting the water they needed and no-one was acting as a look-out.

Everyone heard the single splash but no-one looked up. Each person thought it was just an over enthusiastic attempt to get the water in the container and the air out. It wasn't until blood started filling the containers as well as water that the first alarm was raised.

Vicky was the first to spot it. John jumped back when the scream came from her. It startled him so much that he released his water bottle in an instant flight reaction. He was just about to shout at her for screaming when, one by one, the screams and shouts started to move down the line as the blood moved down until it reached him.

In the confusion Tony grabbed his wife's arm.

"You got water?"

"Yes, it's full" she replied.

"Good."

Still holding her arm tightly he stood and dragged her backwards.

"Tony, you're hurting me, what's wrong?"

As the words left her mouth the air was filled with another cry, but this wasn't the group being startled by the blood that now ran freely down river, this was something ungodly, something none of them had heard and Tony knew it was coming.

"That's what's wrong. Now, with me!"

His wife did as Tony told her.

They had been married for thirteen-years and she had never known a time when she could not trust him.

They turned and headed for the cover of the brush. Pushing frantically through into it, he dragged her down and laid over her in a protective position.

"Stay still and keep very quiet." His words came slowly and forcefully, "DO NOT MAKE A SOUND!"

She lay flat, her face barely out of the soft moss that covered the hard floor under it.

"Tony, you're scaring me, what is it?" Her voice trembled and fluttered as she whispered.

"I heard them last night circling us and they've been following us but that fat bastard's too full of himself to notice. We're going to split and make our own way; it's our best chance!"

Tony looked back up away from his wife's face at the group in front of them. They were still standing in fear, rooted to the spot like lost, frightened prey animals, everyone just looking at each other. The sound came again then another and another, overlapping each time.

Tony's spine ran cold. Whatever was making this noise there was more than one of them. The sound from the group changed from sullen moans of worry and fear to shrieks of absolute terror when the first animal appeared; heading up the river edge from the north at a lightening speed, roaring as it did, its feet pounding into the ground with each huge stride.

The group turned and ran in unison, heading away from it, heading south and away from Tony and his wife. Both of them lay still as the huge feet came into view and then vanished in an instant as it chased down the remaining people they had left the plane with only a day ago. Then the second animal burst through the cover of the tree line it had used as ambush cover directly ahead of them.

Now with the group stopped they had nowhere to run but the second one didn't charge. It just stood and blocked their escape route.

John turned and headed for the cover of the trees. As he did he pushed Vicky as hard as he could, causing the second animal - that was playing sentry - to turn its attention to her as she yelped and protested. She fell forward, her bag landing heavily, spilling its contents onto the river bank as she was sent sprawling into the water. As her phone landed on the hard ground the one touch facility was hit and the video camera came to life.

Its lens looked upwards, capturing the deep blue sky; only slightly obscured by the large green canopy of the trees and neighbouring shrubs.

Its view was soon obscured by the large snout of the first animal that had charged them. Its teeth jagged and razor sharp, the perfect natural knife for carving through raw flesh and bone; they jutted out from its mouth too large and uneven to sit behind the thick lips that were now wet with saliva dripping from its mouth.

From its nostrils two large red crests rose from its skull over its eyes, and the HD video system captured the look in them perfectly; and it was a look of absolute abhorrence.

With a smooth quick motion the head disappeared from the view finder as it dived past it and then came back up. The auto focus struggled at first to home in on the new image but when it did, her own phone recorded Vicky's death.

The animal took advantage while she was attempting to get back onto her feet. She was on all fours, her short-skirted designer suit stopping her making the quick retreat she needed.

Its sharp teeth dug deeply into the soft flesh of her back; momentarily picking her up as it pulled its head back.

She howled in pain, screaming with the absolute agony that

now filled her entire body. Waving her arms and kicking her legs, her body weight became too much for the hold it had on her and a large chunk of her abdomen ripped from her body.

She fell back to the water's edge; still alive but running only on instinct. She reached around her back with her left hand, pain streamed around her body; an intense scorching pain but she couldn't cry for help, she couldn't cry in pain, no air reached her lungs, her lungs were no longer there. Her hand found its way to the empty space where the right side of her rib cage once was, and shook violently as it entered the cavity.

She felt the warmth of her own body and the sharp edges of the broken and snapped ribs that now stuck out of the torn flesh. The phone recorded as the animal raised its head to full height and chewed and swallowed what it had ripped from her. Its head came back down past the view of the lens and as it did the phone's battery died and Vicky with it.

The second animal now charged again driving into the remaining crowd, knocking as many of them over as it could.

Tony adjusted his position, but he couldn't quite understand what happened next. The two animals weren't killing there and then, they were rounding up some of the group, herding them into a smaller, more manageable group.

The two animals then started to circle like a great white shark would circle a seal before charging it from the dark murky depths. Then they changed tactics. They now took it in turn to hit them one at a time, snapping and standing on the legs of them, disabling them, stopping them from breaking out of the small herd and running to get to cover or try and escape, and Tony realised with horror what they were doing.

Once they had immobilized them they stopped and formed a guard around the injured, stopping any rescue or escape attempts, then lowering their heads they bellowed as if to finally warn off anybody or anything foolish enough to try and take their prey away from them. The noise was so loud and menacing it felt as if it was physically pushing the remaining survivors away back into the trees and shrubs that surrounded them. Husbands and wives, forced to leave their loved ones behind, were stopped dead in any rescue attempt by the animals guarding them. Then Tony's heart sank and tears ran down his cheeks as one by one the animals turned and massacred their disabled prey.

Sleep didn't come easy that night for either Tony or his wife; still lying under him. Hiding as best they could, they couldn't sleep because as well as the usual noises that had surrounded them and kept them awake since they had crash landed here, tonight there was a new noise that kept them from sleeping. It was the sound of flesh being torn and ripped from the bodies of the passengers that hadn't escaped and they could hear the bones cracking and crunching as the huge jaws clenched down and shook.

The sounds of soft moaning replaced by screams of pain and agony pierced Tony's ears; he shielded them as best he could but the noises still came in.

Eventually the screaming and tearing stopped, he watched as best he could see by the bright moonlight as the two predators left the scene of the carnage. Their stomachs now full they headed back up the trail. Footsteps thundered past him as he lay as flat as he could; terrified that one of them would see or smell him and his wife as they passed only inches in front of them.

The footsteps eventually faded and the forest returned back to an uneasy truce, the strange sounds of this place now returning to the fore.

Eventually they both fell into an uneasy sleep. Tony woke the next morning with the sun beating down on the clearing where the slaughter had taken place. He eased himself up and quietly woke his wife. "Sandra, Sandra, wake up! I think it's safe and we should go."

She stirred and sat up next to him. "Have they gone now?" She asked him, her voice full of sadness and fear. Tony could see that her eyes were still red and sore from the tears she had shed the night before and he felt frustrated and angry that he couldn't do more to protect her from what had happened.

"Yes, I'm sure it's safe now, we should make a break for it."

They stood up and pushed back through the foliage that had offered them a sanctuary last night onto the trail that ran besides the river.

As they started to head away from their hiding place they passed the patch of ground, now stained red and strewn with the remainder of clothes and human remains. As they did Tony could see the water bottles and canisters dropped in the confusion by the other group members. He let go of Sandra's hand and as he did she grabbed his arm and pulled him back.

"Where are you going?" she whispered.

"We need that water, stay there!"

Tony pulled away again and steadily headed over towards the water bottles; his feet stepping over the remains and through the blood-streaked ground.

The smell hit the back of his throat but he managed to control his gag reflex. The last thing he needed now was to start vomiting because he knew this could attract other predators that could no doubt already smell the rotting corpses.

He was now walking over towards the water bottles. Flies had already started to mass around the open grave; there seemed to be thousands of them buzzing around him. Tony flapped his arms around his head. "FUCK OFF!" he swore at them, gritting his teeth; of course, it made no difference.

Slowly he collected all the water bottles he could see and made his was back to Sandra, who was still rooted to the spot where he had left her.

"Ok, let's get away from here before they come back or worse." "Or worse?" she replied. Tony didn't respond, he didn't need to add to her concerns; instead he lead her away in silence up the trail away from where they were. He knew going back to the plane would be dangerous. Whatever these things were last night they had been following them for a while waiting for their chance to strike and heading back to the plane would take him and Sandra back towards them.

John had run hard and fast after the attack. He had pushed Vicky hard knowing her falling down would create an easy target for them and that would give him the vital seconds he would need to get away. Her screams and cries had chased him through the thick trees and shrubs as he ran, but eventually, of course, they had stopped as had he.

He couldn't run any further. His lungs heaved for what air they could get and a stitch gripped his stomach; doubling him over in a pulsating pain that came in spasms which brought him to the ground.

Resting against the trunk of a huge tree he sat and regained his breath. Distant screams and cries echoed around him, he listened to the terror that was happening from where he had been. He covered his ears and closed his eyes as tightly as he could, hoping to drown out the sounds that seemed to penetrate his soul and haunt him.

Finally, silence fell and the forest returned back to its normal state. He had regained his breath by the time night started to fall and the realisation that he was on his own now kicked in.

In his absolute need to survive the attack he hadn't followed the pack and stuck with them. He had separated, instinctively knowing that breaking away in stealth was his best chance of not being seen, but now he was regretting it. He was on his own, it was getting dark and he knew from his time on the plane and from last night in his tent that it was at night when the strangest of noises started and he had no desire to see what animals were responsible for them, but out here he had no cover, no protection and now he had no group to hide in and no way of making a fire. Instead, he curled up under the tree and tried to make himself as invisible as he could.

Darkness fell and the noises soon followed. Things in the dark moving around him only seemed inches away but he could see nothing, not even his hand held in front his face or the finger he touched his nose with; so he would never see what was out there.

The daytime predators had long since bedded down for the night. This was the time for the nocturnal feeders to come out and hunt. He pulled his knees up tight against his chest and wrapped his arms around them putting his back firmly against the tree hoping this was the best position to ensure that nothing could sneak up from behind. John didn't know how long he had been like this. He had no track of time and he didn't dare illuminate his watch in case it brought unwanted attention, so the night seemed to be unending, the sounds of the forest becoming louder and louder.

The feeling of panic started to swell up inside him. He could feel his pulse increasing, paranoid feelings began to take control. He imagined that something was standing over him, watching him, studying him and that at any moment it would snap down him and pull him apart, piece by piece.

His eyes darted in every direction but there was nothing but blackness. He thrust a punch out, then another and another hoping to strike whatever abomination was standing in front of him, but he hit nothing. The cries of the other passengers came again and the noise their two attackers made soon followed. He knew that the sounds were coming from inside him, the people that he had left behind were long dead. He pushed his hands against his ears as tightly as he could but he could not silence them. He wanted to scream, he wanted to tell everything around him to shut up and leave him alone, that was when he heard the twig snap in front of him. His attention was brought back to the present, all the noises that had haunted him now vanished, and all around went deathly quiet. He heard it again, another shuffle of earth directly in front of him but he couldn't see anything, he was in a pitch black void. Slowly he reached into his pocket and pulled out his phone. Holding the screen tight against his chest he pushed a button on the keypad and instantly the screen illuminated. His breathing had become shallow and his hands wet with the cold sweat that now ran from every pore in his body. He turned his phone to face away from him and held it out at arm's length.

The tiny screen sent a beacon of light into the dark that surrounded him, but he saw nothing. He moved it left and right, still nothing, then the screen went dark. "Fucking thing," he whispered to himself, still holding the screen outwards. His thumb searched for a button and found one, again the screen lit up but this time he saw something.

There was a shape in the darkness, something there but he couldn't make it out. His thumb hit the button again making sure the screen would not go dark again. He moved slowly forward, his eyes squinting, trying desperately to make out the shape that was before him. As he got closer he saw something about it he recognised. "A nostril?" he thought to himself, but that's all he could see or he thought he could see; all around it was still in darkness.

The light died again and his thumb instantly hit the button, but this time it had moved closer to him and now he could make out a snout, he saw the nostril clearly, he could see scales around it and he could see the thick lips just below it and he froze. The snout pulled slowly away from the light and disappeared back into the black void.

John started to release the breath he had been holding since it had come into view, but as he thumbed the key pad and relit the phone's screen, he saw the snout come back into the light, but this time at speed. He had just enough time to see that it was open and now he just made out the huge teeth before the light extinguished again, but the light had not gone out because its time was up on the screen delay. John knew why the light had gone when he felt the excruciating pain that came from his forearm and he realised that his arm and phone were now inside the mouth he had just been able to make out seconds before.

He let out a cry of sheer pain and then felt himself being pulled up and tossed away from the tree. He felt himself become free from the clenching sensation he had felt around his arm as he flew through the pitch black night, not knowing where he would land or how far he was off the ground.

He braced himself for the inevitable impact that would follow and it came hard and it came fast. He landed on his stomach, face down. He felt the damp ground against his face but he could not feel his right arm and realised with horror that his attacker had not released him, but that his arm had been torn off.

Crying and whimpering, John felt the inevitable feeling of acceptance and defeat wash over him.

He could not see anything; he had no idea where his attacker was. He could not run; he could not defend himself, all he could do was lie there and wait for death to come and as that thought passed through his mind the jaws came down again and snapped his neck.

Chapter Eight

William was woken up by Amy. "William," she whispered. He sat up and rubbed his eyes, yawning at the same time, but he took a few seconds to come around. "What?" Was the only word he could muster. He looked up into her face; she was smiling softly at him. "Come on, sleepy we need to go get some stuff."

"Yeah, I'll be up in a minute." He yawned again and stretched out. She moved away giving him enough room to climb out of the seat.

He followed her over to the galley where Marcus and Nick were waiting for them.

"Morning," said Marcus. "Good sleep?"

"Not really," William replied. "I still can't get over them leaving like that and following John."

"I wouldn't worry, in times like these people will follow anyone who says or promises what they want," Nick said.

William nodded, he knew he was right and he knew there was little point in going over it again and again. They had gone, they had made their decision and he had to concentrate on himself and those who remained on the plane.

"I'll go check on Holly," he said.

"Don't be long, William, we need water!" Marcus said. "We'll meet you in the hold."

William watched as Marcus, Nick and Amy headed down the ladder. After they had disappeared he went over to see Sarah and Holly. When he got there Sarah was laid back in the large reclining seat reading a book.

"What's the book?"

She looked up and smiled. "I brought it with me, girly romance you, know?"

William smiled, "How is she?"

147

"Not good," Sarah replied. "She's sleeping all the time now and her arm is really bad, and God, it stinks."

"Ok, we're off out for water can you close the door behind us?"

Sarah put down her book and climbed out of her seat.

"I could do with the exercise, it's not much fun sitting here all the time. I haven't been outside yet."

"There's not much to see, Sarah," William replied. "Besides, we need you here for Holly and the door. Once we're out we can't leave it open."

Sarah didn't reply; her face had a resigned look of agreement across it as well as a little disappointment.

William and Sarah joined the others in the hold. They were waiting by the already open cargo door. The breeze from outside pushed against Sarah's hair; the air smelt sweet and warm and she could feel the sun on her face, but Marcus snapped her attention back and the enjoyment of the fresh air was short lived.

"Ok, Sarah, when we've gone, close the door then make your way to the flight deck. When you see us coming back head down and open it again."

William looked puzzled.

"The flight deck? We going a different way today, Marcus?"

Marcus turned to William, "If we keep heading out and coming back the same way we'll leave a trail, so we need to keep alternating."

William didn't reply, he gestured in agreement and moved towards the door with the makeshift water containers they had made from what luggage was left.

After they had climbed down and Sarah had secured the net and the door, she made for the flight deck as she had been asked to do. Making her way into the cramped cabin she settled into the pilot's seat. The view from here was very different from the seat she had occupied next to Holly since they had landed here. From the front-facing windows she could see right down the clearing as far as the trees on the other side, and the mountains in the distance. From the side windows the clearing seemed to go on endlessly in both directions.

She leaned back and as she did she could see them coming from under the nose of the aircraft. She watched them as they turned a sharp right and disappeared from view. She made herself as comfortable as she could and started to read her book; taking sips from her last remaining water bottle. She could feel the morning sun streaming in through the small windows. Leaning over she slid open the pilot's side window and once again the breeze she had briefly enjoyed in the cargo hold came in surrounding her and wrapping itself around her. She smiled to herself and continued to read.

William was walking next to Amy with Nick and Marcus leading the way a few yards in front of them. They had been walking for around an hour when they came to the clearing that would take them down to the river and the water they so desperately needed.

Stopping dead, the four of them took almost a centurion stance. Checking the horizon in every direction making sure that it was clear, William turned to Amy, "Stay behind me!"

Amy nodded.

"Ok, William, this is your show now, you've been here before, where do we go?" asked Marcus.

William turned to him and Nick, "Ok, follow me but stay in single line against the tree row. When it attacked it ambushed us. We didn't know it was there even with its size, it stayed quiet."

William bit his bottom lip, then continued, "If we see it again, dart into the thickest part of the trees. We can meet back up after it's gone." With that William started to lead them down the trail, constantly scanning in every direction as he did, his ears on full alert for any clues or smells that it might be near.

Eventually they reached the river and William brought their little convoy to a halt.

"Ok, two on look-out, two fill the bottles."

Marcus said, "Me and William will take the look-out!"

Amy replied, "Ok, but remember keep a look-out on the water too."

"In the water," Nick interrupted Marcus.

"You not heard of crocodiles, Nick?" Marcus replied. "You can't see in the water. Look on the surface for tell-tale signs!"

William and Amy nodded back to him in acknowledgement.

Slowly they approached the river. At full stretch they lowered the water containers into it and started to fill them, placing them one by one back on the bank as they did. Amy kept a watch on the surface of the water watching for any tell-tale signs of predators under it.

William scanned the trail looking and listening intently. He could feel the adrenaline rushing around inside him his heart beating fast, he was on full alert and he was damn sure he wouldn't be caught out again.

After what seemed an age to him he heard the words he had been waiting for, "Ok, we're done," said Marcus.

Each taking two containers; the four of them started their passage back to the safety of the plane.

William knew he couldn't relax. Even though so far it had passed without incident or even a sighting, he knew it was when they had relaxed last time they were caught out.

They had made it half-way up the trail; still sticking close to the tree line when they heard a noise. A cry, almost a bark, and William froze.

Marcus moved up next to him. "Is this It? Is this the noise you heard last time?

William shook his head, "No, this is a different one."

"What do we do?" asked Nick.

William placed the water containers on the ground. "Leave these here, we'll head into the shrub line and hide."

"Leave them here? We can't just leave them," Nick protested.

"Unless you can run while you're carrying them you'll have to, they're no good to you dead!"

"William's right," Marcus agreed. "Leave them here, we'll come back; no-one will take them, there's only us here."

The bark came again, closer this time. It was answered, then more joined in and now William could feel the vibration under his feet. He turned to the other three, "Can we go now?"

Placing the containers down, they backed away into the tree line and lay low. The vibrations became stronger, but not as strong as William remembered; the bark came again, then the shadow was cast over them. There was more than one animal, there was a herd, smaller than the one William had seen previously by the water before the T Rex had come, but no less impressive. Walking squat on all four legs they had bony plates running the full length of their backs with sharp ridges that protruded from the sides.

Amy slowly raised herself up and headed back on the trail as the last straggler passed.

"AMY! what the hell are you doing?" William's voice was a mixture of anger and frustration.

When she turned he could see the look of wonderment and excitement on her face as she waved at the three men still cowering in shrub line. "Come see this, it's amazing."

Marcus was the first to raise himself out of the ditch followed by Nick and then William. They joined her and watched as the herd made its way slowly and purposefully towards the river.

"Shit, looks like we made it just in time," Marcus said.

"They wont hurt you, not unless they feel threatened anyway," replied Amy.

Marcus looked at her. "And just how in the hell do you know

that?"

She smiled, still looking at the animals as they turned the corner and started to disappear. "Because they're herbivores, they're called Edmontonia, they're plant eaters."

William let out a little laugh, "Ok, good, we have a dinosaur expert."

Amy laughed with him. "Not really an expert but I know a few of them."

As the last one rounded the corner and vanished Marcus turned to pick up the water. "Come on, boys and girls, it's time to head back."

"Hang on," Nick said. "We have the water, but what about the food?"

"Good point," William said.

"What you got in mind?" asked Marcus.

Nick clenched his teeth and turned to Marcus, "You got your gun?"

"Yeah, but why?"

"Those things that have just passed the Edmo...whatever they are, their heads are about so high."

Nick placed the flat of his hand against his chest, "We can't penetrate the skin but I bet at close range that 9mm would go through the skull?"

"What? You have to be joking, don't tell me you think this is a good idea, Marcus," Amy snapped at him, but Marcus was taking it seriously.

"Look, we don't have any food, apart from some micro crap still in the galley and that ain't going to last too much longer and nor will the power for the oven. We have to eat, he's right."

Amy turned to William; the look of wonderment long gone and now replaced by sadness.

William shook his head, "I don't like it any more than you do, but we have to eat."

Nick shrugged his shoulders. "So, are we or not?"

"If we do," said Marcus, "how the hell do we get it back to the plane? It would weigh a couple of tonnes."

"We don't take it all back, we kill it, take what we need and then leave it," Nick replied.

"Aw, great, Nick, so we waste it as well as kill it?" Amy interrupted.

Nick had a frustrated look on his face. "If we have a rotting carcass under the plane who do you think it will attract?" We're best off leaving what we can't carry as a decoy."

"I agree," Marcus said, "but we'll need to come back. I have no cutting blades with me and we have nothing to carry it in. I suggest we get the water back tonight, eat what's left in the plane and go hunting in the morning when we are prepared."

"I agree," William said, "I think we should head back now."

Amy sighed and turned to Nick, "It's typical, no-one has ever seen a dinosaur and the first one you see you want to blow its brains out and eat it."

"I don't want to," Nick replied, "but if we don't we will die slowly of starvation, you want that? Because I don't!"

The walk back to the plane was a quiet one with Marcus and Nick in front and William and Amy behind them again.

Sarah saw them making their way from the tree line and as she had promised she headed down and opened the cargo door to let them in.

Slowly they managed to get all eight water containers into the hold before she closed and secured the door. Now safely back on the plane, William relaxed and made his way back up to the passenger compartment.

As the light faded and the day gave way to the night they switched on the few overhead lights they needed to safely make their way around the plane. Only the low mutterings between Nick and Marcus in the galley and hum of the microwave oven cooking what was left of the supplies shattered the silence that now fell over the plane.

It was dusk, it was the time when the noises of the day fell away and left an uneasy peace until the night creatures came out.

As the time passed, darkness now completely surrounded them, shrouding the aircraft in a blanket of black nothing.

William made his way through the plane heading for the flight deck, he climbed into the pilot's seat and settled back pulling his blanket over him and pushing the pillow down behind his head. As he turned on his side to look out of the side window he felt a cold draught on his face. He noticed the side window was open and realised that Sarah must have forgotten about it. He reached over and pulled it shut, fastening the catch. He didn't want any prehistoric moths joining him tonight. His eyes scanned the blackness but of course he couldn't see anything of the world outside. Instead he listened and he could hear the usual noises, cries, howls and others he couldn't describe even to himself; but tonight he could hear something else, something was moving around outside close to the plane. He could hear the footsteps and he could hear it rubbing against the metal fuselage. He wasn't worried, he knew they were safe up here but even so he was happier when it stopped and moved away, and only then did he settle down and eventually fall asleep.

Marcus woke William soon after sunrise. "Come on, sleepyhead, we're going shopping."

William didn't reply, he knew Marcus's tone of sarcasm by now and he knew it was best not to rise to it; especially as he had just woken up.

"Ok, Marcus, I'll be out in a minute."

Marcus gave him a heavy tap on his shoulder and headed back towards the galley.

William passed by Sarah and Holly on his way from the flight deck to the galley and both were still sound asleep. He pushed the curtain back to find Marcus, Nick and Amy waiting for him.

"Morning," said Nick. "Sleep ok?" William smiled. "As best as I could, I guess."

"Do we need to wake Sarah up for door duty?" asked Amy.

Marcus turned and replied, "No, I think this time me, Nick and William will be able to handle this. You stay here."

William readied himself for the fight he was sure would follow, but to his surprise Amy didn't challenge him.

"Ok, then, let's get this show on the road," said Nick.

William opened the cover leading down to the hold and headed down. Nick, Marcus and Amy followed him. Once they were by the door Marcus picked up a towel he had placed there the previous night.

"What's in the towel?" asked Nick. As he did, Marcus slowly unrolled it to reveal three hunting knives. Each one had a thick moulded handle that was attached to a long blade, serrated on one side and razor sharp on the other.

"Where the hell did they come from?" William asked.

Marcus smiled. "I had them in my luggage down here."

"And you didn't think to bring them yesterday or even tell us you had them?" Nick replied.

Marcus turned to Nick, "Didn't think we'd need them for water, besides, I had my gun."

William shook his head. "We wouldn't need them? Why wouldn't we need them?"

Marcus didn't answer; he didn't like being pursued in this way and decided he didn't want this conversation anymore and the look that came across his face told the rest of them not to keep pushing. Instead he offered Nick and William a knife each and tucked his into the strap he had put around his right thigh.

After the three men had left and started on their hunting

expedition, Amy sealed the door shut and headed back up to the flight deck to keep watch. This time Marcus led them away from the plane under its right wing; trying again not to leave a definite trail which would prove easy to follow.

Pushing through the thick shrubbery again they came out onto the trail leading to the river. Marcus stopped at the edge of the tree line and turned to William and Nick, "You two ready for this?"

William shook his head, "Not really, Marcus, but if we want to live!"

Nick remained silent. Even though this was his idea, now the time came to carry it out and slaughter an animal, he couldn't help but feel a mixture of trepidation and regret even though they hadn't done it yet.

"Ok, then, let's go."

Marcus set off waving them forward with a large arc of his right arm. The trio pushed on down the trail watching and listening; they were all very aware that while they were hunting they could easily become the hunted. Eventually they came to the place where they had seen the herd yesterday. Today there was no sign of them. They pushed on up the trail towards the river. The sun was high in the sky shining in scattered patterns through the tree canopy. Nick pulled his phone out and checked the time. William sniggered at him, "What time you got then?" Nick looked at William and smiled. "Yeah, I know, force of habit, don't know what difference it makes, anyway the battery is about to die."

William pulled his phone out now and checked it; one bar showing for the power.

"Got you checking yours now!" Nick said. "What's yours showing?" he asked.

"One bar, William replied. I reckon about 12-hours before it bleeps and dies."

Marcus continued ahead of them oblivious to them

comparing their cell phone batteries.

After another hour the three of them turned the bend and came upon the river and then stopped, around 300-yards ahead was the herd.

"Ok, men, this is what we do." Marcus gathered Nick and William close to him and went on to describe the plan - as he called it. Once he was sure they understood he dispersed them off to get ready to flank one of the animals that stood at the rear, if it bolted.

Marcus slipped quietly to the very edge of the tree line that ran parallel to the river. Slowly he made his way towards what he thought was an older animal. It was large compared to the rest but it stood towards the edge of the herd, almost on its own and at the rear of them. As he approached it he pulled the 9mm pistol from its resting place in the back of his belt, gripping it tightly, he carefully and as quietly as possible released the safety catch then cocked the barrel knowing that the first bullet was now in the chamber and ready. He reached the tail; it was thick and immensely strong. Looking at it he could see the muscle definition even through its thick hide. He passed the huge solid rear legs; he could see the side of it moving in and out as it took deep slow breaths, its armour plating expanding and contracting as it did. He got to its front legs. It raised its head and turned it to look at him and Marcus froze, he was eye-to-eye with it.

Marcus could tell it didn't know what he was and why should it? it had never seen a human before. The animal stared at him, squinting trying to work out if this strange-shaped animal was a threat or not. It continued to stare at him as it chewed on his food. Marcus stood perfectly still; any sudden movements on his part now and he knew it would bolt or worse: charge and he knew he would have no chance - not even with the gun ready.

Time seemed to stand still until its head moved back to take another huge chunk of vegetation. "Finally," Marcus thought. He moved again coming slowly alongside its head. He pulled the gun up and steadying it with both hands, he moved the barrel closer to the side of its head. Gritting his teeth he wrapped his index finger around the trigger. The tip of the barrel was now only inches away from its skull and Marcus could feel his hand starting to shake and he knew it was now or never, he knew he had to do it. As if by itself the muscle in his index finger started to tense, curling his finger in until slowly it overcame the resistant of the trigger.

A single shot rang throughout the forest and as the gun kicked back in his hand the large animal collapsed in front of him, lifeless and limp. Instantly the herd bolted. Cries and barks sounded in alarm as they started to stampede away from them leaving their fallen behind.

William and Nick came out from their hiding places and walked towards Marcus. As they approached him from behind he was standing upright with his head bowed down staring at the carcass that lay in front of him; its huge bulk now lifeless and still. He stood with his legs apart and his arms hanging down limply at each side, the gun still hanging from his right hand; smoke still escaping the barrel.

"Ok, now what?" asked Nick.

Marcus turned to him, "What do you mean, now what?" Marcus replied.

"What I mean is, which bit do we take and how?"

William moved closer and knelt down beside the body.

"No, really, Marcus, which bit do we take?" asked William as he looked up.

Marcus laid the gun on the ground, its barrel still too hot to tuck in his trousers. As he stood back up he pulled the hunting knife from his holster and stabbed it deep into the flesh of its hind leg. With the knife standing up out of the leg he turned to William, "We take whatever our knives can cut through and it's not going to be that armour on its back, we take the hind legs and leave the rest."

William stood up and moved next to Nick. They each pulled their own knives out and followed Marcus in the butchering of their kill. Eventually they removed both rear legs and bound them together with vines they cut down from the surrounding vegetation. With the three of them only just able to lift what they had cut off they started the slow walk back to the plane.

Tony and Sandra had followed the trail since they were ambushed. They had drunk and replaced the water they had taken that day, many times, and survived on fruits and berries they had found as they had walked. Apart from the usual noises that menaced them during the day and haunted them during the night, they had not seen any more dinosaurs as they had now resigned themselves to saying. At first they had trouble believing it let alone saying it out loud but now after what they had witnessed they both firmly believed that nothing else could shock them, they hadn't seen any more because they had decided not to walk along the water's edge. They both figured that this would be where their greatest chance of a meeting occurring and because of that it was the best place to avoid.

To replace their water supply Tony would go down to the bank under the cover of darkness and fill the bottles up using a long stick he had shaped to hold them under the water. The sun was high in the deep blue sky. Tony looked up and wiped the sweat that ran freely down his forehead. "Is it me or is each day getting hotter than the last?" he asked Sandra.

"Don't complain, dear, it could be worse," she replied.

"Worse, how the hell could this be worse?"

"Well, if we have somehow gone back in time we could have ended up in the ice age!"

Tony smiled, Sandra always knew how to improve any situation.

"As usual, dear, you're right...of course."

They continued further on until the trail started to narrow and forced them back towards the riverbank and a blind corner that made Tony stop. On the other side of the river the bank rose steeply and vertically up around 15 ft.

"What is it?" Sandra asked him.

"I'm not sure," he replied. "I just have a feeling. There's something. I can hear something. I think we need to cross the river and get up higher."

Sandra started off but Tony grabbed her arm and pulled her back. His grip was tight, almost painful. She turned to scold him over his grip, but stopped when she saw the look in his eyes. The last time she had seen this look was a few days ago when he had pulled her into the bushes before the group they were with were ambushed. Tony released his grip a little and pulled her arm round, guiding her in behind him tight against the tree line that ran along side of the riverbank. He turned and faced her, a look of determination was evident on his face. He raised his index finger to his lips, *"Shhh!"* then moving his finger back he pointed to the spot she occupied and Sandra knew what he meant and then he turned and started slowly ahead towards the bend in the river.

Tony sneaked along the tree line staying as low and as quiet as he could until he managed to round the corner. Sandra watched as he disappeared. She fell back little by little until she was sitting firmly on the ground. Looking around now without Tony next to her she felt alone and very vulnerable, but she knew she must hold it together. She couldn't give in to her emotions and do what she had wanted to do for what now seemed to be a long time, and that was to break down and cry. Just as the feeling to do so became almost too much to contain she remembered what happened the last time people screamed

and cried, and with that image still burning in her mind she
bit her lip and buried it deep down.

Tony cleared the corner, poking through the thick bushes.
He saw what he had felt from where he had left Sandra; there
was a pack of four of them standing five to six-feet tall on
hind legs. Long, strong forearms with claws and long
protruding snouts. Large eyes scanned their environment. It
seemed to Tony that they were taking it in turns to stand guard
whilst the others drank from the river that now flowed faster
than it had only a short distance further back. The guards of
the pack constantly sniffed the air raising their noses high and
sniffing in large gulps before blowing it back out. Tony's gaze
drifted to their feet, and that's when his horror took full
control of him. Set between their claws was a larger single claw
that seemed to be hinged independently to the others and
Tony knew instantly what this was for. He shifted his position
and carefully pushed his way back around the corner until he
was sure he was out of their sight line. He crawled back to
Sandra and sat beside her. She could tell by the look on his
face that he had seen something that terrified him.

"We can't go on that way," he whispered to her. "We need to
cross the river and get higher up and then we might have a
chance."

"What's there?" she asked him, but she really didn't want to
know and she certainly didn't want the answer he gave.

"Raptors," was all he said and she knew enough about
dinosaurs from the movies and documentaries to know that
one wrong move on their part and it would be over for them.

"Have you got your phone?" Tony asked her.

"My phone?"

"Yes, Sandra, your mobile phone, you have it or not?"

She nodded and passed it to him. He pressed the key pad and

instantly it lit up.

"Thank God it's still charged."

Sandra shook her head. "What are you doing?"

He turned to her whilst changing some settings, though she couldn't see what they were.

"We need a distraction, and this is it!"

He looked around and found a piece of wood big enough for the phone to sit in. Slowly he inched his way to the water's edge and placed the wood with the phone on it in the river and gently nudged it and then returned to Sandra. The floating decoy - now in the middle of the river - started to flow downstream and around the bend towards the Raptors. Its 21st century casing of piano black and bright silverwork; contrasting sharply against the dull dead wood that now carried it away from them.

Tony looked at his watch and started to count down: 5, 4, 3, 2,1.

Suddenly Sandra heard the phone come to life. Its LCD screen lit as the mp3 player started and her favourite band began to sing. 'Mr Blue Sky' filled the air and it was instantly joined by the protests of the Raptors.

"Genius!" Sandra smiled at Tony.

"You can thank me later, if this works."

He grabbed her hand and set off for the river. They ran as fast as they could through the cold icy fast-flowing water. A thousand needles instantly jabbed at their legs as the water soaked through their clothes. They could feel their muscles being drained as every step became harder than the last.

They were half-way across now. They knew they had to make that final push, they had to reach the other side and get up the bank to be safe. Tony could see the animals now from where they were. The Raptors, still puzzled by this thing that had invaded their privacy and silence, jabbed at the water. He pushed on, pulling Sandra with him. His legs became heavier like the dreams he had had as child growing up; he would try and run away from something, something that would terrify him even though he never saw it, but his legs wouldn't move; stuck fast to floor or in thick treacle. No matter how hard he tried he could never run. Then he would call out to his mother and she would rescue him. She would tell him it was a dream, tuck him back into bed and make him feel safe. But not now; this was real and she wasn't going to wake him from this, she couldn't save him this time.

He pushed against the water; his feet fighting for a grip against the smooth slippery stones that covered the bottom. He had another look. The Raptors were still engaged in the hunt, for now they were ok.

Tony's hand made contact with the mud bank. He took hold of the roots that were sticking out of the wall with his right hand and pulled Sandra to him with his left. His arms and legs ached, his chest heaved and his breathing was laboured but he had to make it up the wall. He knew they were not out of danger yet. Taking hold of anything they could use as leverage they scrambled their way up the bank until they reached the top. Panting heavily they lay on their backs; the hot afternoon sun warming them and bathing them in an almost recharging glow.

The sound of the Raptors splashing the water and barking still carried on even though the phone had sunk below the surface and become silent, but he knew enough about wind direction and the way it carried scents to know that up here they could neither see them or smell them.

Tony turned towards Sandra, "We made it!"

A few minutes passed before he regained his composure. Turning to lie on his front he now had a full view of the river and the Raptors that seemed to be still occupied with the strange item that had spooked them. Two of them were still dipping their snouts under the surface to try and find it and he decided they must have been juveniles because the larger animals of the pack had given up and now barked at them as they turned and headed away in to the trees. Instantly the two in the river gave up and followed.

"Ok, then, go get my phone back!" Sandra said with a smile.

"Yeah, right."

Tony and Sandra stood and walked along the top of the bank; the cold water now becoming a lost memory as the heat of the sun found them out in the open. Up here there were no trees to provide shade and for now Tony and Sandra were happy to walk hand-in-hand with the sun for company.

It wasn't too long before they had the answer as to why the river was gaining speed. Before them was a sheer drop, to their left a waterfall where the river ended and no doubt the brave little phone's journey would have come to end had the Raptors not sunk it when the music had started. To their right the cliff edge ran as far as their eyes could see and straight ahead of them was a valley. In the distance on the opposite side of the valley - almost as far as the eye could see - the skyline was dominated by a volcano. A mountain range ran in a circular pattern down both sides, ultimately meeting the cliff where they stood. Below them the valley was a fertile green carpet. What looked like birds circled above it, and in the middle was a huge lake where Tony decided the waterfall must eventually run into after it had weaved its way through the trees. As the sun shone down into it they could see different shades of green that made up the canopy and in the clearings below them a multitude of different coloured plants and flowers. After the dense jungle and ragged riverbanks it seemed to them that they had reached some sort of sanctuary in a place were fear and death were constant travel companions.

He took hold of Sandra's hand and gently squeezed it.

"There really is no way out, is there?" Sandra's voice sounded tired and defeated, her face had a look of inevitability about it.

"No, this is it, Tony, this is where we are."

"What do you think they'll tell the family?" Tony asked.

"Once they realise the plane is missing they'll probably make up some story of a crash with no wreckage or survivors. Let's face it, the truth will never be known," she answered.

"What now, then?" he asked.

She turned towards him and let go of his hand, pointing down in to the lush valley that stretched out before them, she spoke softly, "We go find somewhere safe to live, for as long as we can!"

Chapter Nine

The camp fire was now nothing more than glowing embers. William, Marcus, Nick, Amy and Sarah had sat outside this evening while they dined on one of the rear legs they had managed to get back to the plane, but as the sun started to set and the atmosphere of this strange environment started to change, they had decided not to relight the fire, but instead let it die out as they climbed back into the safety of the plane.

The remaining meat was left outside and none of them were particularly happy with this, but given the only other choice was to let it rot inside the cargo hold it seemed the best idea.

Sarah was the first to climb inside followed by Amy.

"Do you think we should move the other leg?" asked William.

"Move it where?" replied Marcus.

William shook his head and waved his right hand around pointing generally anywhere away from under the plane.

"I don't know, Marcus, but should we really leave it here?" he replied.

Marcus looked at the leg and then out around their darkening surroundings. William had seen this look before and he knew Marcus was weighing up the options.

"I don't think it would be a good idea to go dragging it out away from the plane now, it's almost dark and to be quite honest, we don't know what exactly might be looking at us right now, but at least here we have some safety."

Nick agreed with Marcus. "It's not ideal leaving it here, but Marcus is right; its better than wandering out there."

"Ok, we'll leave it till morning," William replied to both of them. He knew they were right but he also knew leaving it under the aircraft was equally as dangerous.

William was the last to climb in through the door. They pulled the cargo net in and winched the large metal door shut. William pushed the metal locks in place and sighed with relief. He knew once they were locked they were safe and only then could he truly relax.

"Good hunting today, men, time for a good night's sleep." Marcus's parting words, as he climbed up the ladder into the galley, rang a chord with William. He felt exhausted and it had been a long day. He climbed up last and dropped the hatch into place. Nick was standing in the galley leaning against the racks of cupboards. The sun now hung low in the sky and its bright orange glare penetrated the closed blinds on the windows; bathing the interior in a soft glow that contrasted with the few remaining overhead lights that they had left switched on since they had landed.

Amy moved through the passengers' compartments. She noticed Sarah - who had settled back into her usual position next to Holly - who had now been asleep for two days. She pushed on through the curtains, noticing Nick and William deep in conversation. She made her way onto the other side and into the economy cabin. As she did, Marcus emerged from the toilets and made his way to his bunk. He gave a courteous smile, as if he was slightly embarrassed about her seeing him coming out of the toilet. She smiled back and carried on with the routine she had adopted almost from the first night here. She walked the length of the interior checking that all the doors were secure and all the blinds were pulled down as David had instructed them to do before he was taken.

Satisfied with tonight's inspection she started to make her way to her own bunk in business class. She wasn't far away from the galley when everything inside the plane went dark as the last remaining lights were starved of the power they needed and the low humming noise that came from the generators slowly wound down to silence.

Amy stopped in her tracks. Nick and William joined her from the galley. "William, what's just happened?" Amy asked in a startled tone. "Well, at a guess, Amy, I would say that the on board generators have finally given out and that there is no more power left!" "Welcome to the stone age," Nick added.

Amy made a sarcastic laughing sound at Nick's reply. "Yeah, you're funny!" she said.

The evening light was just enough to illuminate the cabin for only the very basic navigation. Marcus appeared through the gap that lead to the galley. "Power's out then," he said as he joined them.

"So now what?" Amy asked him.

"Well, we have the lanterns from the camping equipment, they're battery powered and may last a few weeks if we're really careful with the usage," Marcus replied and then continued, "I would suggest we use them to get bedded down and then switch them off."

"What about a fire?" asked Amy.

Marcus smiled at William and Nick. "I'm not saying anything to that," he said with a slight laugh. "If the plane burnt out we would be completely unprotected and vulnerable," William said.

"We have another problem as well," Nick added.

"What's that?" asked Marcus.

"The toilets were powered by the generators, so now they've gone as well, and of course the heating for when the winter comes." He paused..."If it comes."

"Let's just deal with the lights and toilets first, we can sort the heating out when and if it starts to get cold, but for now it's getting too dark to do anything. I suggest we bed down before it gets pitch black."

Marcus replied, "Ok, I'll take the flight deck tonight and let Sarah know what's going on with the power," William said.

Amy eagerly agreed. She didn't like the dark even in the

comfort of her own home let alone on this plane stranded in this place. She followed Marcus and Nick through to business class and settled down just behind Marcus as Nick headed again for the captain's bunk. William closed the flight deck door behind him and made himself comfortable for another night of restless sleep.

He wasn't sure how long he had been asleep. When he awoke it was still dark; pitch black in fact. All he could make out were the droplets of rain on the windows that were illuminated by the large moon that hung over them in the night sky. As his eyes slowly adjusted he could see further past the windows. He could make out the outline of the trees and the large foliage that skirted around them. The rainwater reflected off the leaves giving them an almost French polished appearance. He could see shapes swaying back and forth as the wind - that had picked up during the night - pushed them one way and then pulled them another. He adjusted in his seat, pulling his blanket further up and rubbing his eyes; yawning as the sound of rain tapped against the metal roof and thick glass and the sound of the wind whistled as it ran around the smooth curves of the nose. For what he was convinced was the first time since they had landed here he started to feel quite restful, he could even feel a smile starting to spread across his face. His stomach was full and he was warm and comfortable whilst outside the wind and rain kept the normal sounds that came at night quiet. He decided that whatever creatures they were they too were keeping out of the storm, but as always in this land his feeling of satisfaction was short lived.

He noticed movement out of the corner of his right eye, first. The shrubs that glistened now seemed to shimmer and the trees swayed, but not with the wind as the rest of them did, they seemed to move against it. Slowly he turned his head round to the right and stared as hard as he could. Something was there, just on the edge of the clearing but he couldn't quite make out the outline. William reached over with his left hand and slid the small pilot's window open. The sound of the rain and wind instantly increased but then another sound came and it was one William recognised: a dull thud followed by another and then a low resonating growl.

William snapped the window shut and then froze in his seat. The sound of his heartbeat seemed to become louder and louder. He placed his right hand on his chest as if to quieten it down. He kept his breathing to short deep breaths, he was simply terrified. The dull thuds became louder and more frequent as the animal broke through the tree line and got closer to the aircraft and as it did its outline started to take shape and William's worst fears were confirmed as the T Rex crossed the front of the plane and walked past William's side window.

He couldn't move; he was rooted to the spot. He followed its progress with his eyes, turning them in their sockets as far as he could. He watched it stride past him and as the back of its head passed over William's shoulder and out of his vision, he found the strength he needed and slid out of the pilot's seat and headed for the door. He exploded through it and then collapsed against it pushing it closed. He felt at any moment the T Rex would burst through the door behind him and he would be powerless to escape.

He looked down the business class compartment; everyone was asleep and then the silhouette appeared in the closed blinds of the small windows. It passed next to him, within inches only the thin metal and glass separated them. He dropped to the floor and made his way crawling past the seats. As he did the outline of the huge head just outside kept pace with him, but he knew he would have to wake his friends. The last thing they needed was for someone to wake up and panic he was sure that if the T Rex heard a commotion inside it would have the strength to puncture a hole in the side of the plane and whilst it probably wouldn't be able to get in, the hole it would leave would allow something smaller in.

William reached Sarah first. He raised himself up by her side and watched as the Rex passed by her window and continued down the fuselage. "Sarah." William whispered her name and gently shook her. "Sarah, wake up." As she opened her eyes William placed his fingers on his lips, *"Shhh!"*

Sarah looked confused. "What?" she whispered back to him.

He pointed down towards the back of the plane and gestured her to follow him. She slid out of her seat and followed William while he woke Amy and Marcus.

"What about Nick?" asked Amy.

"He's asleep in the captain's bunk and there are no windows in there. He should be ok if he stays asleep," replied Marcus.

"Yeah, if he stays asleep," interrupted Sarah.

"I think he's the lucky one, it passed inches by him and he slept through it," Amy said.

"Where is it now? I can't hear it anymore," Sarah said.

Marcus looked at William and gestured to him to follow. The two men pushed through the galley curtains and made their way down the economy class towards the centre of the plane.

"Its shadow has gone," William said.

Marcus pointed further down the cabin, "No it hasn't."

Suddenly the image of its massive head appeared again against the closed blinds.

"It must have walked around the wing," said Marcus.

They watched as its head dipped down under the windows.

"The meat, shit, it's here for the meat," William said.

Marcus looked at him. "We have to do something, we have to scare it off or it will come back again and again looking for food."

William grabbed at his arm. "Scare it off, how the fuck do you intend to do that? That gun you have won't even scratch it!"

Marcus smiled, "No, but the flares will...follow me."

He led William over to the hatch that led into the hold. Grabbing one of the lanterns they climbed down into it.

"I must be fucking mad," William said.

"No, William, not mad, if this works we won't see it again!"

Marcus lit the lantern and made his way to the door. The cargo bay looked foreboding, lit only by a single lantern. Shadows and strange patterns filled every unlit area that the little lamp couldn't reach and William expected the Rex to leap at him from every one of them even though he knew it couldn't possibly fit in here. But knowing that it was outside the door made the atmosphere down there even more terrifying and his imagination was running away on his fear.

As they approached the door both men knew that the Rex was only a few feet away from them; separated only by a few thin inches of steel. Marcus pulled the safety catch across and started to wind the handle that dislodged the door and cranked it open.

After it was open by only a few inches - just enough for Marcus to get his head and shoulders out - he stopped and locked it in place. "Ok, switch the lantern off," he ordered William.

William did as he was told. He was in no position to argue or even think against anything Marcus would say. Right now all he could concentrate on was survival. Marcus pulled the flare gun out of his jacket pocket and smiled, "Wish me luck, William." With that he lowered himself and slid his head and upper torso out of the door.

Marcus was met with a moon-filled night sky. Dark massive clouds passed by it and he could see the rain droplets running down the curved fuselage and further away the trees glistened and gleamed. The large green leaves wet with the rain reflected the moonlight back at him against the black velvety background.

He turned his head to the left and then he saw it, or at least he saw its legs. Two immensely strong legs and leading back from them, a colossal tail that swayed back and forth. Marcus tried to pull his arm around to line the flare gun up to aim, he wanted to hit it in the middle of its back. He thought that that would be enough to send it running and not come back. He twisted his body round and started to bring his arm up alongside him to take his shot. His hand managed to get most of the way up his side when the gun snagged against one the hinges on the door. He turned his attention away from the Rex for just a moment to re-adjust his position and free his arm. He released the stuck flare gun and turned back towards his target; the rain now ran down his face and in to his eyes. He blinked furiously to clear the water from them, and when the clarity came back he realised the Rex had moved and now they met eye-to-eye.

Marcus froze, he had the flare gun free but it still wasn't lined up where it needed to be; he looked at the angle of the gun and then instantly back into the eye of the Rex. Its small eye stared at him intently. Rain ran from its face down its thick curling lips and onto the huge sharp jagged teeth, that now seemed to be getting closer and closer and bigger and bigger.

Marcus blinked hard, clearing the rain once more, but the Rex was still there still staring, still snarling. Marcus heard the low grumbling that came from the back of its throat and it sounded exactly as he imagined it would when William had described it after it had taken David. His attention was brought back in an instant when the grumbling turned into a definite growl. Marcus made his decision, he brought the gun round to line up the shot. He would direct the flare straight at the Rex's eyes. It all seemed to happen in slow motion, from the thought in his brain to the nerve impulse sent to his muscles to start the process of moving his arm and eventually pulling the trigger.

He watched as the gun moved through the rain, and Marcus began to scream hoping to stun and confuse the Rex, allowing him the seconds he would need to get the shot away.

In the cargo bay all that William could see was Marcus's waist down to his feet, all he heard was the scream as his arm moved, pulling the gun to line up the shot, but he didn't hear the flare leave the gun and he didn't hear anything else from Marcus after his legs disappeared through the small gap he had left in the cargo bay door so quickly; that William didn't even get time to react and try to get to them.

William screamed after him but it was no use, he was gone and when he finally gained the courage to peek through the small gap all he saw was the back of the Rex as it headed away and back into the moonlit emptiness that surrounded them.

Instantly, William cranked the door shut and secured the thick locking bar. He headed back up to the passenger cabin. Hysterical, he clambered up the ladder and fell in to the arms of Amy, who had been waiting for them, he didn't say anything to her, he couldn't, no words could form his sheer anguish, but she could see clearly by his face that something terrible had happened. He fell against her and sobbed. Amy cradled him but knew there was nothing she could do to make his pain and sorrow go away and just as she thought that night could be no worse, Sarah came through into the galley and through her own tears and sobbing she announced, "It's Holly, she's dead!"

Chapter Ten

Bruce had spent the time, since he had returned to his tent, trying to get any information he could from the flight recorders, but it was useless, both recorders were blank; their hard drives corrupted so badly that not even the powerful retrieval software that he had could piece together any bits of information.

He sank into his chair and stared at the screen of his laptop, the cursor just stared at him occasionally blinking waiting for his next command but he had none to give. He tried to piece together the clues he had about the flight, the two reconstructed faces, names that were mentioned in the diary and of course the body itself.

Andrea had checked the body for ID but to no-one's surprise there was none. Over time the survivors must have changed clothes and no doubt as they had come to accept that there was no chance of rescue and that they were in fact alone, why would they have kept their ID in a safe place or even carried it with them?

Bruce lowered his weary head into his hands, he was tired and even though he wouldn't admit it, especially to Simon, he was beaten.

Mustering what little energy he had left he raised his head and checked his clock, the green illuminated numbers read 8:03pm. He sighed heavily, he knew that Susan and Andrea would be here at any moment along with Simon to go through the rest of the diary and unless it gave any further clues to the discovery of the plane and its passengers; it was game over and that above everything was what Bruce feared.

As he sat in silence, Susan and Andrea came into his tent, he looked up from his chair and greeted them with a resigned look on his face, forcing only half a smile. As he did he said

175

nothing but simply gestured towards two camping chairs he had put out for them. Susan sat in the one closest to him.

"You ok, Bruce? You look really down."

His smile widened. "Taking everything into account, Susan, I would say I'm just great!"

His answer was delivered with an almost aggressive undertone and Susan didn't really know how to respond in case she rattled him further.

She turned to Andrea and shook her head. Andrea spoke to him next. "You seen Simon since this afternoon?"

Bruce was already regretting the way he had just spoken to Susan, he knew as the words were delivered the way he had spoken to her was not right and as if to try and apologise and ease his conscience he engaged with both of them in much more civil manner. "I haven't, Andrea, I assumed he had returned to the plane to keep an eye on Mark and the forensics that your team is doing, Susan." As he spoke her name he looked directly at her and smiled, and she knew that this was Bruce rectifying his last comment.

She nodded to him and replied to his rhetorical statement, "No, Bruce, I was over there myself most of the day and I haven't seen him." As she finished her sentence the tent flap pulled open and Simon came in. "Hi, sorry I'm late. I just had to finish off something," he said as he made his way in and sat down, but Simon had an uneasy look about him as he had earlier and now Bruce could see it as well as Susan and Andrea.

Susan looked over at Bruce and he could see a look of concern about her face; something didn't feel right, they all felt it and before Susan was willing to carry on reading the diary she wanted it clearing up. "What's the matter, Simon? You've been quiet most of the day, and missing to come to think of it?"

Simon shifted in his seat with an anxious smile, desperately trying to hide the look of utter guilt he had been wearing when he came in. He looked up from his seated, position around to Susan first, then Andrea and finally up to Bruce who was now standing at the foot of the chairs and has he did they could see his expression change. "I got a call today from the guys that took the metal sample from the plane, you know, the metallurgists," he said in a soft voice.

"Ok, good, go on," replied Bruce.

"That's the point, Bruce, it's not, they rang me to tell me that while the sample was being looked at, it was found to contain something that couldn't be identified, there was a change at the molecular level of the metal."

Bruce looked at Susan and Andrea, and in turn they looked back at Bruce and all of them had the same expression of confusion and imminent dread on their faces.

"Go on, Simon," Bruce urged him to continue.

"Well, when these things come up there are procedures, lines of command that have to be followed."

Bruce interrupted, "Yes, and?"

Simon shifted again, his hands were clasped tight between his knees and until then his head had hung low between his shoulders, but now he raised it to face is colleagues.

"They reported it to the CDC and the NSA."

Bruce's expression changed again, it wasn't imminent dread now that Bruce felt and showed it was very real dread and he could feel himself becoming angry.

"So what does that mean for us then?" He pushed Simon for the answer even though he already knew it.

Simon took another deep breath. "The call was a tip-off." He paused..."he told me they're on their way here now and are expecting to arrive around 11:00 tonight."

Bruce flew in to a rage, "Do you know what that means? Do you? For fuck's sake, Simon what were you thinking? They'll shut us down and bury the whole fucking thing. We will never find out who these people were, their families will never have closure." Bruce spun round, he needed to vent his frustration and the closest target was his work station. He took hold and with all his strength tossed it over as hard as he could. The flight data boxes and laptop took the brunt of the impact, smashing against the thin groundsheet. The laptop exploded into a hundred pieces of plastic and circuit boards.

Instantly, Susan jumped from her seat. "Bruce, Jesus, calm down, he's done nothing wrong, it wasn't his fault, you knew this would get out at some point."

Bruce didn't reply, he turned back to face them and stared directly at Simon.

Susan continued, "Look, it's only 8:30, we have some time on our hands, we may be able to at least determine the flight or the company; we might still be able to find the truth and solve this."

Bruce slowly sat on his camp bed, his temper now burnt out. He looked over at the broken pieces of his laptop and the data boxes; now lying on the floor, and then back to Simon. "Look, I'm sorry, Simon. I know it wasn't your fault, but..." he didn't get any further, he stopped mid-sentence and this time it was Simon who cut across him. "I know, Bruce, but I called them, I brought them in."

Bruce nodded and looked back to Susan. "Our only real hope is that diary, I think you should start to read it again."

Susan looked back across at Simon, "You ok now?"

Simon smiled at her and nodded before gazing back down at the floor. She looked back at Bruce and gave him a strong look of disappointment, as if to scold him for taking his frustration out on Simon, and Bruce knew. This time he didn't get in to a staring competition, he just looked away.

Susan sat back in her chair and pulled the diary from her pocket...

We lost Marcus and Holly two days ago, the fever took Holly. Finally she gave in to it. I guess she wasn't strong enough but at least she didn't suffer; she drifted into death from her sleep. I suppose it's how we all want to go, if truth be known.

It was different for Marcus, he was taken by the same bastard animal that took David. The T Rex. It came looking for the food we'd left under the plane and he died trying to scare it away. It comes every so often. None of our phones or watches work now so we're not sure but we think every six weeks or so, when the moon is full.

It hasn't come back up to the plane but we can hear it moving around outside at night, and if the moon is high we can see the trees tremble when it moves past them, but the biggest sign is the deathly quiet that falls over the place minutes before it arrives, it's as if every other living creature here hides: including us!

Susan looked back up from the diary, "Look, I think this can tell us a lot about the day-to-day stuff, but right now we need clues." She started to skim through the pages looking for anything that might tell them something that could give them a head start on the agents that were now on their way. It was towards the back when she stopped, and Andrea could tell she had found what she needed; Susan looked up at them, "Listen to this..."

I'm on my own now. Sarah was lost today and in this place those odds are un-winnable, so I've decided to end things on my own terms. Those evil godless bastards are not deciding how it ends for me. If, by some miracle, anybody does read this I hope you understand why I did what I did and you won't judge me too harshly.

The funny thing is, I didn't need to be on this flight. I only went to that damn meeting to hand in my notice; to tell them where to stick their fucking job!

I left Portland expecting to be at Atlanta and then home again in three days! I don't know how long we've been here now exactly; we lost track of the time a long while ago. We just lived day-to-day. We watched the seasons change, the winter isn't that cold but the summer...God, it was hot too hot for Nick; he couldn't take it; it wasn't the creatures that got him: he got himself!

"Stop!" Bruce yelled. "That's it, that's what we needed to know."

Susan closed the diary. "Portland to Atlanta, we have the pilots' names; all we need to do is marry the airport, pilots and airline together and we can give their families some peace before the NSA bury it!" he said.

Andrea replied, "We can do more than that; there is a good chance this flight may not have taken off yet; we may be able to stop it!"

Bruce looked at her. "What? Of course it's taken off; the damn thing is over there." He pointed in the rough direction of the dig site.

"No, she's right," Simon added. "If this plane travelled back in time and excluding all the logical explanations; that's what happened, it might not even take off until next year or the year after."

Bruce spun his gaze back to Simon. "What the hell are you talking about?"

Simon stood up, that schoolboy look of excitement slowly returning to his face as it had the very first day they had arrived here. "Bruce, how many planes do you know that are currently missing, presumed down?"

Bruce thought for a second, "None!"

"Exactly, if this plane had already taken off and was already missing we would know about it. The fact we have not received any alerts means it hasn't happened yet."

Susan backed him up. "They're both right, we still have time to stop it."

Bruce stood up and held out both palms towards the excited

group as if he was trying to slow an approaching car. "Look, even if this Star Trek stuff was right - and I'm not yet convinced - all we have is an airport and the pilots' names."

"Yes, but we can deduce from that, we can contact the air companies who fly form Portland and find out which ones have pilots called David and Steven and air cabin called Holly and Lynsey. Christ, it's worth a shot! If we can stop this happening then the changes to the metal and how the plane survived for so long won't matter!"

Bruce pulled his mobile and flipped open the case. "No signal, now what?"

Without warning a loud crack came from outside the tent and a flash of brilliant light illuminated it. "What the hell was that?" Andrea shouted.

It came again and then the sound of rain started to hit the tent. "That's fucking great, not a drop for weeks and when we need to make a call we get an electrical storm!" Bruce shouted, his look of frustration now apparent again.

"We can drive there," Simon said. "It's what? a few hours from here and if we take turns we can make it in one go." The four of them looked at each other and then bolted from the tent.

The wind outside had now risen. Dust and sand flew around the tents and their feet, swirling up, making small independent twisters; no taller than a small child.

Cups and plates from the kitchen tent flew around them and the untied flaps of the tents protested and flapped in the strong wind, slapping against the canvas and guide ropes around them. "Get to the car! I'll be there in a minute," Susan shouted to them.

Bruce, Andrea and Simon made their way to one of the Landcruisers that was parked at the edge of the main entrance to the site and climbed in. Bruce got in the driver's seat and checked for fuel while Simon climbed in next to him. "We ok for fuel?" Bruce turned and smiled, "Our luck might be changing, we have a full tank and keys!" He turned the ignition and the engine purred into life; the headlights lit up and the sand now swirled and danced in the glare of the brilliant white light.

Susan finally jumped in next to Andrea. "Where did you go?" asked Bruce.

"Needed to tell Mark to expect the NSA and CDC and to give them what they wanted...slowly!"

Bruce laughed, "Ok, then, here we go."

He shifted the car into drive and planted his foot down on the accelerator, instantly the 2-tonne truck sprung forward; its four-wheel drive digging deep in to the desert sand for traction and as it did its red tail-lights disappeared into the dead of night.

The drive to Portland was a long one; over 900-miles, non-stop and it took its toll on all of them. Even taking it in turns and stopping for fuel on four occasions, it had left them exhausted; they had continually tried to call ahead but the electrical storm they hoped they would leave behind in Death Valley had followed them all the way.

It was a massive system and even the car's radio had been knocked out by it, they had no communication the entire journey, only now as they approached Portland itself the storm system started to clear and the radio and mobile phones started to come back to life, but by now they were there, now they didn't need them.

Bruce was back at the wheel after taking over from Andrea at the last fuel stop. He hurled the large SUV through into the drop-off zone at the airport, desperately looking for a place he could abandon it so that they could stop the plane and stop the series of events that had already happened millions of years ago, and now even though they were almost there and they had explained it to him over and over again on the journey there, Bruce could still not get his head around the premise that the plane they had left on the desert floor could still be on the tarmac right here, right now, but his thoughts and concentration were brought crashing back by Susan.

"BRUCE!" Her shrill yelling snapped him back but it was too late, the taxi was already in front of him and he had no time to react. The Landcruiser hit the front wing of the taxi and pushed it like a child's toy across the tarmac and back into the parking bay it had tried to pull out of. In an instant the front of the SUV lifted and mounted the taxi where it came to rest. Bruce - dazed and shaken - turned to his passengers, "Everybody ok?"

Susan and Andrea nodded.

He turned to Simon, who waved at Bruce to get out the car. Bruce climbed out through the half-open door and onto the bonnet of the taxi. The driver shouted at them to come back. Pinned by the crushed door and his deployed air bag they left him and the wrecked taxi behind with the Landcruiser still mounted on its bonnet.

The four of them pushed past the queues of people who were making their way into the airport. They were desperate to try and solve this puzzle and ultimately stop the events from ever happening.

Simon tripped over a man trying to get out of his way and pushed him against the handle of the door. Swearing at him in retaliation, the man tried to push Simon back but he wasn't quick enough and Simon left him straddled against the door.

They pushed on through the airport and made their way towards the administration section. "Stop there!" a voice boomed from behind them.

Bruce spun round to see an airport police officer catching up to them. Bruce - now almost exhausted and resting his hands on his hips - pulled his ID badge from his pocket. Through short breaths he greeted as best he could the officer who had now caught up with them. "Hi, Bruce Ackland, I'm a lead air crash investigation officer with the NTSB. I need to see the airport manger immediately."

The officer had a sideways and dismissive glance at Bruce's ID. "Listen, I don't care who you are, for now all you're going to see is my holding room; the four of you come with me!"

Bruce moved closer to him and removed his hands from his hips to allow him to stand up straighter. "Listen, I need to see the manager and I need to see him now!"

The officer matched Bruce's stance and both men found themselves almost toe-to-toe, but Bruce knew from the guard's physique and the look in his eye this was one he couldn't win and backed down to try a different tack.

"Look, officer, I know, the car outside, but this is very important, let me speak to the manager then you can sort out whatever you need to, please?"

The officer relaxed, almost in reflection to Bruce, "Follow me," was all he said as he started to lead them away.

As Simon started to turn he noticed the man that he knocked over at the door, his impulse was go and apologise but this time he knew he couldn't; even though he hated the idea of someone walking round thinking he was discourteous or worse: some sort of a thug.

On the walk through the private corridors of the airport, the parts the public never get to see, the security guard informed the duty manager he was on his way and who he had with him.

The officer led the four of them into the duty manager's office. "Sir, these are the people I told you about. This is the air crash investigation officer, I'm not sure who the other three are."

The manager looked up from behind his desk. "That's fine,

officer, I'll call you when we're finished here; can you please arrange to have their truck removed and that taxi towed as well?"

The officer - that had all but frog-marched them to the office - turned and left, closing the door firmly behind him.

The manager stood up and introduced himself. "Hello, I'm Michael, I'm the duty manager for the night shift, who might you be?"

He was a polite man, he reminded Bruce instantly of all the political types that he had to work with and report to that he hated so much. He had been in the desert now for what seemed an eternity, surrounded by tents, sand, dust and heat and he'd been so focused on the plane and the mystery around it that he had almost forgotten about the concrete and chrome world he actually belonged to.

Bruce extended his arm forward, "I'm Bruce, this is Simon, Andrea and Susan."

Michael nodded and gestured for them to be seated and settled back behind his desk. "So, Bruce, tell me, what is it that's so important you feel you can crash your truck outside my airport and run through it like some half-assed recreation of Die Hard?"

Bruce didn't respond straight away. He wanted to, he wanted to reach across that flatpack cheap desk that was planted in the middle of this grey dull office, grab him by his cheap tie and shake some sense and respect into him, but he knew he couldn't, he knew this was a job for diplomacy; this couldn't be sorted by shouting and banging, so he drew a deep breath and started to explain the events that had brought them all to this point and the reason they had come to his airport tonight.

Time seemed to stand still while they did their best to convince him to take their story seriously, but it was to no avail.

Bruce knew from the start that Michael - like all the rest of the corporate clones - would not listen to them. He wouldn't take their story on face value and nor would he act on the information they had given him.

After three hours of trying their level best, he simply asked them to leave, promising that he would look into it and report back to Bruce if he came up with anything and Bruce knew as he shook his hand, he would never hear from him again. And so exhausted, they walked back through the airport towards the entrance. Bruce stopped and looked out of the viewing gallery windows, he could see the aircrafts taxiing, taking off and waiting for their passengers to board them. Simon joined him by his side. "Imagine, Simon, it could be any one of those planes out there, it's enough to send you stupid."

Simon didn't reply to Bruce. He put his arm around him and gently pulled him away from the window and followed Susan and Andrea as they headed back towards the parking area; where they could retrieve their car for the long drive back to the dig site; where they knew the government agencies would simply shut them down, remove the plane and deny it ever existed.

Chapter Eleven

Twelve years had passed since they had landed in this place. Twelve years since William had lost everybody around him, except Sarah, who had survived with him throughout this time.

Ten years since Amy had been lost to a stampede of Stegosaurus that had bolted when they had tried to hunt using the 9mm that Marcus had left in his bunk the night the Rex took him. The shots that rang out from the gun had startled them. Amy was fast and she ran as quickly as fear itself could carry her, but she wasn't quick enough and her screams of panic - and then of pain - still haunted him to this day.

It had been six years since Nick had died; this time not by a dinosaur or some other freak of nature that William hated so much, but by the simple act of a heart attack. Even here amongst all these monsters and dangers in a place with a million ways to die, it was a heart attack, a 21st century killer that got him and to William, in a perverse way, it brought him comfort to know that some things could remain constant and familiar. They had buried him with Steven and Holly, they had said some words, but both of them knew now for sure that no God could be responsible for this place.

It was another winter's morning that they had woken to. The sound of the rain rattled against the now dull and scratched bodywork of the plane. In some places mould had taken hold of the cream and beige roof lining and the windows were streaked and dirty, but it didn't matter to them, they never opened the blinds now; the only light that got in was in the flight deck or when they went out for food and water. They had to take it in turns now, there was no-one left to operate the cargo bay door, and they still didn't dare leave it open. In the last couple of years a new menace had come to call on them, when the T Rex wasn't around the Raptors were, and they feared them even more than the Rex.

Today it was Sarah's turn, they headed down into the cargo hold and William winched the door open, throwing the net out after it. "You be careful out there," he said as Sarah started the climb down. "Don't worry, I'll be back in no time to annoy you," she said back to him, smiling.

Water collection no longer involved the journey to the river. They had managed to rig a pulley system in the larger of the trees that surrounded the plane. Now they lifted the water containers up on a rota basis allowing them to fill with rain water, it was the hunting that took the time now, but today was just water and both them felt very relieved that it was.

Visibility on these dark cloudy days was not good and once you were in amongst the trees it nearly became night and then it became unnerving almost to the point that starvation was preferred to going in there at all.

After Sarah had climbed down, William closed the door and made his way to the flight deck. He watched her leave as he had countless times before. He watched as she disappeared in to the jungle and he didn't move until he saw her come back out. As soon as he did he bolted down into the cargo bay and started to wind the door open. As always, she was standing waiting for him, her usual smile and deep blue eyes were a welcome sight. He lowered the cargo net down and started to pull the first of the two water buckets into the hold. He took hold of it and pulled it up in to the cargo bay. Placing it to his right he leant back down for the next one; Sarah was reaching up with it. She was at full stretch, the container was almost within reach when a dark shape passed quickly from under the plane. Instantly, Sarah dropped the container she was holding up for him; it fell backwards rolling away under the plane and the water escaped. Sarah set off after the container. He didn't see the shadow, he was convinced she had just tripped back from the net. If he had seen it he wouldn't have let her go after the container, but then he saw this dark shape flash pass the fuselage and in an instant he heard her cries. His heart sank and immediately he knew what was happening. He reached behind his belt and drew the pistol that they had kept. Pointing it out of the hold he pulled the trigger, hoping that the noise would scare off her attackers. Four shots rang out before the barrel cocked back and chamber was empty but it didn't stop them. He froze holding the now useless gun, still in the air, pointing it up, his mind overloaded as the screams of David, Marcus and Amy came flooding back.

Sarah's cries snapped him back and he dropped the gun. Smoking, it fell to the ground and as it did her screams became a gurgled cry for help as her own blood started to choke her.

Still half-hanging out of the cargo bay door desperately trying to locate where her cries came from, William felt a sharp pain in his hand. He pulled it back towards him instinctively and he realised it was a Raptor that had jumped and struck out with its forearms. He looked in horror as two of them now ripped and pulled at the net that still hung out of the open door and onto the ground. He pulled against them as hard as he could, his adrenaline now giving his muscles as much power as they could but it still wasn't enough. The two Raptors snarled and barked as they frantically tried to get to him. His hands sweated, he couldn't pull against their weight and he knew if one of them made it up he would stand no chance. He had one more chance to get the net, one more thing he could try.

Reaching across he pulled the last remaining flare gun from its resting position by the door and fired it directly at the lead Raptor. The red hot flare hit the animal head on and with an unearthly cry it let go of the net followed instantly by the second one.

189

William pulled the shredded net in as fast as he could, his arms were tired, he was exhausted; every sinew of him ached and wanted to quit, but he knew he had to get the door down, he had to get the plane locked and secured or his fate would be that of Sarah's.

Sarah, his thoughts turned back to her, her cries and screams had long since stopped. He knew she was dead and he knew that he could do nothing for her; just like he could do nothing for all the others that had died before her.

In the noise and chaos a thought shot into his mind; clarity came to him and all around him seemed to be a dream. Would it be so bad to give himself to these monsters that were now clawing and scratching at the fuselage below him? How long would it take for them to rip him to pieces if he just jumped down now? He still had his knife, he might even be able to take one of them with him.

He looked down at the creatures that baited him, their sharp serrated teeth set in long protruding snouts that foamed and curled, their excitement and euphoria at the thought of him as their next meal was making them become frenzied, like the sharks he had watched feeding in documentaries, except this time the bait was him.

He snapped back to reality again, he noticed their strong forearms and those claws on their feet. Instantaneously he was filled with revulsion and disgust, the dream state switched back to the clear and brutal reality he was in. No, if he was to die here it would be on his terms, his way and with that he wound the cargo bay door shut and pulled the safety catch across, collapsing back onto the floor. He could still hear them scratching at the metal but he knew he was safe. He regained his breath and composure. Standing up he made his way up the ladder into the galley and placed the hatch down. Locking it into position he went into the galley, dressed his wound with a clean white handkerchief and poured himself a cup of water from the last bottle he had up there.

His mind was clear. Now the Raptors knew he was here they would never leave, and that meant he could never leave, they would starve him out, he would run out of water and food and in here - in this 21st century piece of technology - he would die a slow painful death.

"Not me," he thought to himself. "If this is my time then so be it, but it'll be easy and it'll be nice."

William made his way through the plane from the rear of the economy class, clearing and tidying as he went, just as he had done before he had left his flat all those years ago. Eventually he reached the captain's bunk and the flight deck, and as with the rest of the plane, he made sure nothing was out of place. Once he was satisfied he made his way to Sarah's bunk. She had stayed in the same bunk after Holly had passed away, he was never sure why and never got round to asking, but he found what he went there for, it was the book she had brought with her to pass the time and she must have read it now hundreds of times. He smiled as he picked up the worn book, holding it close to his nose he smelt it through deep breaths and it smelt of her. A warm smile spread across his face as he remembered her laugh, her smile. He stopped and slowly lowered the book down, the smile evaporating from his face as her memory started to fade and he made his way over to his bunk.

Night was starting to pull in, he could see the changing shapes and patterns through the blinds and as it did the Raptors gave up their siege for the night, but he knew they would be back in the morning, but by then he also knew it wouldn't matter anymore. He reached into the overhead locker and took out the note he had prepared some time ago when Sarah had been out collecting water. He settled into his bunk pulling his blanket up and pushing his head back in to the deep soft pillows and he felt at ease for the first time since that afternoon in his apartment while he'd been waiting for the taxi; as the sun glowed through his window and bathed him in its warmth.

He felt serenity and he had a clear mind. At last he knew what was going to happen, he knew he didn't need to make instant decisions he didn't need to react, to think on his feet, depending on what was around the bend or how the weather was. He was in control and it had been a long time since he had felt that.

He took the tablets from his pocket that he had taken from Sarah's bunk, they were what was left from treating Holly. Sarah had stopped giving her the tablets long before she died when she had realised that using them on her would eventually prove to be futile. Tipping them in to his open hand he stared at them. Then without any hesitation, he placed them all on his tongue. Taking a gulp of water from his cup he pushed his head back and swallowed them all at once. Leaning to his left he placed the cup carefully into its holder. He didn't want to spill anything, especially now, he didn't know how quickly the tablets would work and he didn't want to go while trying to clean up a spill!

William opened Sarah's book and started to read it in the low sun of the early winter's afternoon; as his eyes became heavy and he felt himself become weaker he allowed his arm to slide down, the book slipped away from his eyes his hand still clasping it as if it was his last link to Sarah. His body started to become lighter; a warm feeling of well-being washed over him and all the memories of his life started to fill his mind: his childhood Christmasses, visiting his long-since-gone aunts, uncles and grandparents. His little red trike flashed through his mind but it was all replaced by Sarah's smile and he started to smile. As he did his eyes closed, and his hand fell open.

Chapter Twelve

Mark watched as the NSA and CDC choppers landed at the edge of the site entrance. Four men wearing what looked like standard issue men in black suits climbed out and made their way over to him.

The wind was still blowing hard and the sky was completely black; no stars could be seen and when the rare glance of the full moon could be seen it showed only huge cloud formations that covered it again just as quickly as it appeared, but the air was now still and electric, it felt charged and Mark was convinced a lightening storm was coming.

His years in the field working under Susan had taught him when to expect one and to treat it with respect when you were out in the open.

"Are you Mark Watson, sir?" shouted one of the men.

"I am and who are you?"

The man showed Mark a black folding wallet with a shield set in the back cover. "I'm agent Smith with the NSA, sir, you have orders to show me to the crash site."

Mark pointed over to one of the parked Landcruisers and shouted at them so he could be heard over the wind. "It's a bit of a distance from here, we should go in the truck."

Agent Smith nodded and gestured to his colleagues to follow him. Mark climbed in the driver's seat. "It won't take long to get there." He turned the truck round and set off for the hangar. Agent Smith sat next to him in the passenger seat and Mark felt very uneasy with him. As the truck approached the hangar the huge blue structure came into view; the massive orange lamps inside made the whole thing glow against the darkened night sky. "Hell of a storm tonight, I'm surprised you still flew in," Mark said as he pulled the truck up.

Agent Smith didn't respond, he simply climbed out of the car and headed into the hangar followed by the other agents. Mark slowly followed them but stopped as he reached the door. Looking up at the sky he noticed something, in the distance far off. He saw a white dot, it looked almost like the landing lights of an airliner but he knew it wasn't; it was too far away.

Suddenly the light began to expand. Mark brought his arm up to protect his eyes but the intense brilliant white light flashed across the sky and then disappeared in the time it took him to cover his face and with it the cloud base vanished, returning the night sky to its normal star-filled magnificence. Mark stared at the sky and shuddered. He felt uncomfortable, he couldn't describe it but something felt out of sync, dismissing it, he turned and headed inside the hangar.

Bruce and Simon had returned to their offices. Three days had past since they had left the dig site and the government agencies had taken it over and as Bruce had predicted, nothing was coming out, no information and no leads. He knew deep down the plane would be removed for scientific testing and any mention of it would be flatly denied. As for the diary that Susan had kept: *the ramblings of a delusional mind* is what they had already decided the official line would be. Scribbled words from someone who wants nothing more than attention and he knew that with the government and all the resources at their disposal, the diary was worthless.

Bruce returned to his paperwork, filling in endless reports and spreadsheets. He rubbed his eyes and sat back in his chair sighing heavily. The events of the past few months had left him physically and emotionally exhausted. His hunger for the job now had gone and with every passing day that was to come he knew he had reached the end of his career. Nothing he investigated now would ever hold the surprise or challenge that he had had.

"Bruce!" Simon's voice echoed.

Bruce sat back and waited for him to come to his office, he knew he would and saw no point shouting back to him. Simon entered holding a report sheet. "Bruce, I think this is it."

Bruce put his pen down and took the paper from him.

"This is what, Simon?"

Simon smiled. "Read it carefully, Bruce, it's a missing report, a plane was reported missing, now look at the flight crew names."

Bruce scanned down the sheet for the information Simon pointed him to, and he froze.

"What did I tell you?"

Bruce pulled the paper away from his face and looked up at Simon, "The names on here are the names from the flight in the diary," Bruce said.

Simon nodded, "Yes, and not only that, the body Andrea worked on, his DNA was sufficient to get a name and he's on the passenger list."

Bruce stood up. "Anybody else know about this?"

Simon shook his head, "Not yet, no, I've called Susan and Andrea, they're going to meet us there."

Bruce looked puzzled. "Meet us where, Simon?" he asked.

"The John Doe, his name was William Relford and we have an address!"

Bruce's expression changed from puzzlement to enthusiasm. A broad smile fixed across his face, "So let's go!" Simon said.

Simon and Bruce pulled up outside of the address he had managed to get from the airline and waiting for them was Susan and Andrea. "Morning, boys," announced Susan.

Bruce smiled. Though it was only a few days, it seemed to Bruce much longer since he had heard her voice; they entered the apartment building and made their way to William's door.

"So, how do we get in then?" asked Andrea.

Bruce turned to her and smiled, "Like this." Bruce put all of his considerable weight behind his kick, and the front door gave in immediately. Bruce and Simon entered followed by Susan and then an apprehensive Andrea. "You can't just kick your way in, Bruce," she said in her usual scornful manner.

"I just did, Andrea, and remember, William's not likely to be back, is he? If we can find something we might be able to…"

Andrea cut across him, "What, Bruce? might be able to what? You still don't get it, do you? You can't stop this, you can't change it. If you could we wouldn't be here."

Bruce looked frustrated. "What the hell are you talking about? Of course we would."

"No we wouldn't. If you had stopped it, the plane wouldn't have killed the dinosaur, and when Susan dug down nothing would have been in that spot, and because of that she wouldn't have called your office and we wouldn't have gone there and met and none of the events that have led us to this moment would have happened!" She finished and sank onto William's wingback chair.

The mood in the apartment changed and Bruce now had to concede defeat. He turned to Simon, "Ring the flight control, ask them when it disappeared."

Simon pulled out his phone and turned to talk to them. Bruce sat in silence and watched as Andrea sat looking out of the large corner window. She turned to Susan, "Imagine right now, 65 million years ago, the man who should be sitting in this chair is living the life we read about in his diary."

Susan smiled but it was a smile of polite acknowledgment mixed with inevitable sadness. She had heard what Andrea had said but the thought of them living through the events that had been documented in his diary left her feeling empty and sad for him. Sad for a man she had never met yet she knew how he lived, how he died, and now she stood in his home, and as the feeling began to smother her she felt the same as she had the night they had climbed into the plane and found his body.

Bruce noticed Simon coming back into the room. "So, what did they say? When did it disappear?" he asked him.

Simon folded his phone and pushed it into his jacket pocket. He turned his attention to Bruce. Simon's face was washed-out, pale and gaunt, "It was when we were at the airport, Bruce. He hesitated and then continued...

"It was 72-hours ago!"

~ Yesterday's Flight ~

CPSIA information can be obtained at www.ICGtesting.com
261778BV00001BA/1/P